CHARGE IT TO THE GAME

Real B*tches At The Table

NAI

URBAN AINT DEAD PRESENTS

SOUNDTRACK

Scan the QR Code below to listen to the Soundtracks/Singles of some of your favorite U.A.D titles:

Don't have Spotify or Apple Music?
No Sweat!
Visit your choice streaming platform and search URBAN AINT DEAD.

Currently on lock serving a bid?
JPay, iHeartRadio, WHATEVER!
We got you covered.
Simply log into your facility's kiosk or tablet, go to music and search URBAN AINT DEAD.

URBAN AINT DEAD

Like & Follow us on social media:

FB – URBAN AINT DEAD

IG: @urbanaintdead

Tik Tok - @urbanaintdead

SUBMISSION GUIDELINES

Submit the first three chapters of your completed manuscript to
urbanaintdead@gmail.com, subject line: Your book's title. The
manuscript must be in a .doc file and sent as an attachment. The
document should be in Times New Roman, double-spaced and in size
12 font. Also, provide your synopsis and full contact information. If
sending multiple submissions, they must each be in a separate email.
Have a story but no way to submit it electronically? You can still
submit to URBAN AINT DEAD. Send in the first three chapters,
written or typed, of your completed manuscript to:

URBAN AINT DEAD
P.O Box 960780
Riverdale GA., 30296

DO NOT send original manuscript. Must be a duplicate.
Provide your synopsis and a cover letter containing your full contact
information.
Thanks for considering URBAN AINT DEAD.

ACKNOWLEDGMENTS

I almost never do acknowledgments in any of my books, but I felt like this book called for one. The last few months I've been on a journey of rebranding and stepping outside of just being an author. For a while my mindset had been, just write the books and the people are gonna come. Well, honey I'm on book 20 and I haven't scratched the surface of where I'm headed. I wanna thank the people that stayed down on the journey. Shoutout to Vee and Katori for keeping me encouraged and staying on my neck. Big thanks to my sis, Andrea for always seeing the bigger picture and not playing about promoting me, lol. Lastly, and certainly not least that man, that man. Shoutout to the man that's gonna be the inspiration around the couples y'all are gonna read about in my books going forward. Ooouu, y'all better get y'all some hood love. Hell, write a book about it so we can go on the journey together.

Yours Truly,
"The Hood Love Dealer"

PROLOGUE

"This game wasn't meant to be ran by a woman," my father told me as I sat across from him in the visiting room at San Quentin State prison. "It's male dominated just like anything else in this world and that's why you gotta be five steps ahead. You come from my loins, so you already have an advantage. I raised you to be a strong leader and never take no for an answer. Your poise and resilience will play a part in your takeover. I'm passing the baton to you and it's going to fuck up the heads of a lot of people but don't concern yourself with idle chit chat. Keep your womanly mannerisms. Just because you're the boss don't mean that you have to act like a man. Stay the course and do this shit right... the Wright way."

I took in everything he said, soaking the words up like a sponge. I knew what was being asked of me and I had no intentions on letting my father down. I had to act like a woman while thinking like a man. Stepping into the shoes of Curtis "Coolie" Wright wasn't going to be an easy feat, but my daddy didn't raise no hoe. With my Queens by my side, we were sure to shake up the city.

"I hear you, daddy. I'm gonna make sure they never forget your name. It'll be like you never left," I assured him.

"They never forget a Legend, baby girl. You just make sure they know the new First Lady at The Table." He reached across the metal table for my hand and squeezed it. It was a sign to let me know that he had to go. Since he started serving his sentence, we had the whole visiting thing down to a science. We never said goodbye because it was too final for me. Instead, he squeezed my hand and I'd say, "until we meet again," and he would nod his head and smile. After doing our ritual, we both stood.

"I love you, daddy."

"I love you too, daughter. Go out there and make me proud."

CHAPTER ONE – MAHOGANY

One Year Later

I sat at the head of the conference table in one of the office buildings I owned with my best friends, Tiffany and Morae to the left and right of me as we conducted the monthly money meeting for The Table. We each listened as the heads of each borough gave account of what they needed for their re-up as well as handing over our portion of their profit. Everything was going smooth until we got to Briscoe. Briscoe had control of Brooklyn. His cocky ass couldn't take the fact that I now ran the entire operation. It didn't help that we were ex-lovers. Since I'd been put in position, he made sure to never miss an opportunity to act like a dickhead.

"This nigga," Tiffany whispered as we watched Briscoe play on his phone as if he didn't know it was his time to report. "Ay, Briscoe, I don't know if you think the concept no longer applies to you, but time is money. And right now, you wasting it. Report, nigga," she pushed.

"Oh, it's my turn?" He played dumb. Reaching down, he picked up an MCM book bag off the floor and sat it on the table. "That's seventy bands." Morae got up and snatched the bag off the table before proceeding to the money room to count it. Like Tiffany, she was tired of his bullshit too.

Over his shenanigans and blatant disrespect, I leaned forward and folded one black, gel- manicured hand over the other before speaking. "You've wasted five minutes of my time that I can never get back. I'm gonna need you to go ahead and add five thousand to your monthly payout. That's a stack for each minute wasted." The smirk he had on his face was now gone.

"Oh, you fining niggas now over bullshit? Get the fuck outta here Mahogany. The way I'm out here bringing in money and you tryna lil boy me?" He stood in a threatening manner and from the corner of my eye, I could see Tiffany place her gun on the table.

"All of this huffing and puffing over five G'z, Briscoe? Damn, I'm disappointed in you, baby. I suggest you pipe the fuck down though; you know how Tiff gets when she feels I'm being disrespected." Slowly, he sat down, and I knew by the slits in his eyes he was embarrassed and pissed about it. I gave not one fuck because he had brought it on himself. "Trick, you're up."

I listened as Trick, who sat to the left of Briscoe, gave his report while Briscoe stared a hole in the side of my face. From day one, he didn't respect my position. He thought that by my father treating him like a son when we were together, he was being groomed to be next in line. He was sadly mistaken because I always knew the operation would be handed over to me if something happened to my dad. It got under his skin that he had to answer to me, a woman. I held the power for him to keep getting money in the city.

"Aight, meeting adjourned," Morae spoke after reentering the room. "Same time next month fellas. If for any reason you need to re-up earlier than your scheduled time, you know where to find me." With no further words spoken, everyone got up to make their exit. As usual, once everyone cleared out, the ladies and I debriefed. I didn't let Briscoe get by me though.

"Aye Briscoe," I called out to the angry man, "you're forgetting something." Tiffany smirked when he turned around. Digging in his pocket, he counted out fifty $100 bills and placed the blue faces on the table. I watched as he ran his tongue over his teeth before pushing the money towards me. I knew he wanted to say something but opted out of it. "Thank you, love." He nodded his head and walked out. Nobody's ever always happy with the boss.

"You need to let his ass go. That nigga so envious of you, it don't even make no sense," Morae said as we debriefed and put away the monthly take.

"I agree with Mo. He wants yo' position bad," Tiffany added. I knew they were right, but the only thing stopping me from cutting Briscoe off was the fact that he did bring in money—lots of it. Although he acted like a bitch behind me being over him, he hadn't snaked me on the business side. I couldn't say that I knew how long it would last though.

"I hear what y'all saying and trust me when I say I'm keeping an eye on him. Briscoe may envy me, but he knows betta than to cross me. He loves his family too much." In the Wright organization, we were big on loyalty and didn't allow second chances when it came down to it. You crossed us, we let everyone close to you feel it and leave you alive just so you could live with the fact that you were the reason for their demise.

"Look, I'll never tell you how to handle business, but I'm telling you the longer you let that nigga live with that malice in his heart, that shit is just going to fester. And that's going to be bad for business," Morae spoke again.

I looked over at her and smirked. "You just want to kill him, don't you?"

"Oh, please, please, please." She had her hands up in a praying motion while she bat her eyes. "I promise not to make it messy."

"Our friend is really looney," Tiffany joked, walking out of the vault while I shook my head and followed.

"Nuts I tell you." I laughed and Mo rolled her eyes at the both of us.

"Y'all never let me have no fun, it's cool though. And how you gon' call me looney when you practically live at the shooting range?" She closed the door behind us and locked it and I looked over at Tiff.

"Hey, I have my thing and you have yours." Tiffany shrugged her shoulders and smirked. I loved my girls. Tiffany was my God sister and we'd known Morae since we were ten. Still in our twenties, we had made a name for ourselves in the game. Morae, Tiffany, and I were three different women that bought different skillsets and personalities to The Table which enabled our business to be such a success.

Tiffany was my beautiful, head of security. With a pretty face, stacked body, and a keen sense of style, one would never peg her as anyone's protector. What people didn't know was that Tiffany was just as deadly if not deadlier than most of the killers I knew. Growing up a military kid, Tiff knew her way around guns. It wasn't uncommon for her to have us at the gun range at any given time, testing out some new shit.

Morae was head lieutenant. She ran all of our spots and ran them with an iron fist. Cold as a motherfucka too. While each borough had its HNIC, such as the guys that were gathered tonight, before anything got to my ears, it went through Mo first. She was my eyes and ears on the ground. Couldn't nobody get to me until they went through her. And even then, Mo had the answers because she knew how I was going to step at all times. A petite thing standing at 5'5, Mo had the shape of an athlete.

She stayed in the gym, toning, but maintained her feminine energy. It was likely why she attracted both women and men but preferred to play on the same team. I pondered everyday why she chose to lick cat as opposed to having a hard dick. To each's own though. More than the skillsets they brought to The Table, I knew for a fact that my bitches were some riders. They would go to war with an army behind me and I knew I didn't have to question the love or loyalty they had for me.

The game was treacherous, and in order to survive in it, you had to have people who were gonna step behind you, no questions asked. I had that times two, well three if you included my father. Shit, even behind the wall, if Coolie wanted you touched, you got touched. Those bars didn't mean shit. As for me, I was the team's all-around player, keeping things running like a well-oiled machine in the background.

To the world, I was Mahogany Wright, the woman behind the infamous "Elite Palace." A popular gentlemen's club in Westchester, NY. I had the baddest bitches, and the niggas came from far and wide to be a part of the "Elite Experience." There was something for everybody at Elite, though. We didn't just cater to the men.

While I had a host of beautiful women who worked in my club, my premiere dancers made it so that it was the talk of the city. Cherokee, Bad Ass Bri, Kat, and Paris were handpicked by me and Morae. We'd done a good job because not only did they make the niggas spend bands, but they were also trained to kill any mother-fucka that was a threat. I ran my club just as I'd run The Table in many ways, with a strict no bullshit policy. I didn't allow drugs in my establishment unless I was the one supplying them, and it was never anything hard. I supplied edibles and free hookah. If you wanted a different high, you could purchase any exotic weed of your choosing or X.

"Are you going into the club tonight?" Mo asked as we walked to our cars. Daylight savings had rolled around, and it was darker than usual for it to only be eight o'clock.

"Not tonight. I promised Beautii I'd be home after this meeting. She wants me to take her out to dinner, said she needs to talk to me."

"If Beautii don't go head," Tiffany laughed. "My girl wanna talk over dinner. I swear she is you all day." It was true, my nine-year-old daughter was a mini me. She had my face and my mannerisms down to a T.

"Yeah, that's my baby so you know I gotta make it happen. What y'all getting into?" Using my remote starter to start my Porsche Cayenne Coupe, I walked around the driver's side to get in.

"After I make sure you get home, I'm gonna take it in for the night. I don't feel like being around a crowd and you know tomorrow is brunch with my dad. I gotta be up and before time."

"And alert," I reminded Tiffany.

"As fuck. You know he don't give a bitch a break. What about you, Mo?" Tiffany asked Morae whose head was in her phone. "Mo!" Tiff yelled out to get her attention.

Mo's eyes shot up and annoyance was written all over her face. "You ain't have to do all that. And yeah, I'm gonna swing by the club a little later to see Paris."

7

I smirked, opening my door to put my purse inside. "You are smitten by that girl."

"I ain't smitten by nobody. I do fuck with her heavy though," she called herself correcting me.

"Girl, that is just the hood definition of smitten." We all shared a laugh, and she waved me off.

"I'll hit the chat once I make it to the club," she said and went to hop in her car. Beeping the horn twice once she started it up, she drove off into the night.

I didn't mind Mo dating one of my dancers because we had long ago set boundaries. She knew she couldn't hoard Paris when she was on the clock and there was no PDA on the floor. I was big on not mixing business with pleasure and Mo respected that. I also lead by example which was why I made sure to separate how I felt about Briscoe from the business.

"You ready?" Tiffany nodded towards me.

"Yeah." I climbed into my car and connected to my Bluetooth to call Beautii.

"Hey, mommy," she answered, not letting the call ring fully.

"Hey, sugar, were you waiting by the phone?"

"Yep. Are you on your way home?"

I smiled and shook my head. "I am, so you can start getting dressed. Where's Gran?" I asked about my mother.

"In the kitchen, reading."

"Okay, I'll see you in a minute. Be dressed when I come through the door, Beautii."

"I will. Love you, mommy."

"I love you too, my girl." Ending the call just as Tiff pulled up next to me, I rolled down my window.

"You down to put some speed on yo' baby tonight?" She was referring to my car. We had pulled up to the meeting in the same car and cracked up at the coincidence.

"Not tonight, Tiff. Let's just get home."

"Ahh, okay. I knew you was scared I was gon' dust yo' ass. Go head and pull out, I'm right behind you."

I smirked and gave her the finger. Truth was, I didn't feel like racing because the girls' comments were on my mind. Briscoe was showing his ass and the last thing I was gonna tolerate was him thinking he was above The Table. I'd hate to have to put my daughter's father under it.

CHAPTER TWO – MORAE

♫ "Doing one hunnit on the freeway, that's what you got me doing these days. Your love so good, it's like I see things, that pussy like I won the sweepstakes. I pulled up on you in a drop top and hopped out baby, front door I'm locked out baby. You right at the door to let me in, you ain't wearing nothin' but your skin..." ♫

Mk xyz's "One Time" crooned through the speakers of my Porsche 911 as I made my way to the "Elite Palace." My girlfriend, Paris, had put me on to the song a few weeks ago and I couldn't get it out of my head. I don't know if it was the lyrics or the sexy tone of the singer, but it bumped. It was crazy how Paris resembled the singer too. Thinking about her and the lyrics to the song, a sneaky smile crept up on my face.

Paris and I had been seeing each other for a little over six months now and I had to admit that she was growing on me more and more every day. I'd be the first to admit that I wasn't the friendliest person in the world, and I wasn't quick to give anybody my time. Both my time and my energy were precious, so to be able to get either was a blessing to whomever. As for Paris, she was able to get close to me by simply being herself. She didn't throw herself at me and to be real, she wouldn't have known that I was attracted to women had I not told her. That wasn't information that I just put out there. And I didn't carry myself as the poster child for bisexual women.

I was just Morae, and I liked what I liked. Growing up in a house full of boys, on the outside looking in, one would have thought that I was destined to play for the same team, but my upbringing had nothing to do with it. I was both a tomboy and a girly girl. Both my mother and father accepted that. They didn't see anything wrong with me wanting to play football with my brothers in a face full of make-up. They encouraged me to be me. My mother wasn't your average woman either.

She was a stay-at-home mom who didn't mind getting her hands dirty when my father was out working. I was the oldest of four siblings. I had three brothers, Maurice, Montez, and Monroe. Of the two of my parents, my mother was the disciplinarian. My dad mainly enforced her rules. Even with her being the disciplinarian she knew how to follow my dad's lead. Overall, she was hard but knew when to be soft. We'd lost her a year after my brother Monroe was born; two days after his first birthday to be exact.

She had a heart condition that she'd been battling for years that only those in our household knew about. My parents were strong believers in, "what goes on in our house, stays in our house." Even with her illness, my mother never slacked on her duties as a wife or care-taker to us. If anything, my dad fussed with her to take it easy. She did, but it wasn't for too long. She'd ease up for a few days then be right back at it.

We all took her death hard although she'd prepared us for her passing. She wrote us each a letter of instructions along with her final words. In her letter to me, she told me that I wasn't allowed to mourn her death past five days. That shit seemed harsh but as I read on, I understood. She further explained that with her being gone, I would now be the glue. My brothers and my dad were strong, but I was the glue that held everything together, just as she did.

I'd been doing that for the last 16 years. It ain't always been easy but always worth it. I loved my family and that included my sisters too. I'd put my life on the line when it came to Tiff and Hogany without a doubt. My phone rang, interrupting the song just as it got to the chorus. Seeing my youngest brother's name on the screen, I answered.

"What you need, Monk Man?"

"Wassup, sis."

His voice was so damn deep with a distinct rasp. People often thought he was a grown man. Monroe was 17 years old and looked every bit of 21. He'd moved in with me a year ago because he and our dad were always clashing. With my dad getting up in age, I decided to take on Monroe full time to allow him to be retired in peace. I also didn't want my dad to have to shoot the one on one with his son. So far, it had been the best decision and their relationship was in a better place.

Monroe was a smooth talker, just like our brother Montez. They were two peas in a pod, and I often had to remind Montez of Monroe's age. I didn't want Montez's whoreish lifestyle to rub off on our baby brother. The both of them wanted to be pimps so fucking bad. They respected women though.

I didn't play that shit and neither did our dad. My dad took care of business when it came to our mama, and he did the same with his new wife who I didn't get along with at all. Definitely a story for another time. All in all, we expected the guys to have that same energy when it came to their women once they decided they wanted to take someone serious.

"Wassup, what you need?" I repeated.

"Nothing, just checking in on you."

"Well, I'm good. Just left the monthly meeting a little while ago, headed to the club to see Paris. Did you complete the task I gave you earlier?"

"Yeah, it's done. Everything checks out. I did a soft and hard background check. I did some digging into his family history too." Monk Man was a whiz with computers and into that dark web shit. Sometimes we used his talents for The Table.

Recently, Trick had put a new runner on his team, and he'd gotten caught up on a narcotic's charge during a domestic dispute. The dummy had been riding around with product on him and got pulled over after getting into a fight with his girl. Trick claimed to have taken care of it, but the last time I pulled up on his trap, ol' boy was in full swing. Confused and baffled, I had Monk Man complete a background check before I made my next move.

"Okay, cool. How about that paper for your history teacher?"

"I put it on your desk, in your office."

"Thorough as always. What you getting into tonight?"

"I wanted to slide to this party the team throwing for the W we got yesterday against Academy Prep." He was a division one basketball player at his high school and could ball his ass off.

"So long as the house isn't in disarray, you can do as you please." I pulled into the club's parking lot and parked on the side where it was less crowded.

"It's just the way you left it, and whatever I used in the kitchen, I made sure to clean. Ummm, can I use my car tonight?"

"Do you plan on indulging at this party?" I wasn't naïve to think that my seventeen-year-old brother didn't drink and smoke a little weed when he was out with his friends. My thing was that he be safe and honest.

"I'll probably have some punch, nothing crazy though. And I'm cool on the smoking if I don't have my own shit."

"In that case, don't ask me no stupid shit like that. Getcho ass in an Uber. What time the party end?"

He sucked his teeth. "The flyer say two."

"Cool, Scooter will be there at one to scoop you, anything else?"

"Man, I don't need nobody to pick me up. I'm good, Mo."

I pulled my visor down to check my makeup and satisfied with what I saw, I pushed it back up. "It can be Scooter, or it can be me, you choose."

"Can you see if Money can get me?" He tried bargaining for our brother to pick him up instead.

"I guess you'll see who'll be there at one. Make sure you're protected and tell Chantel's fast ass the next time I see her on my camera walking around in a t-shirt and her panties, Ima whip her ass. Enjoy the party, I love you."

He snickered. "Aight. Love you too and I'll text you when I get there." I ended the call and grabbed my Chanel purse off the seat and my Beretta out of the glove compartment. Tossing it in the bag, I got out ready to see my baby.

"Hey, babe," Paris spoke as she walked off the stage after her performance. I admired the way the light hit her skin, making the glitter on her body sparkle.

Paris wasn't as thick as the other dancers. She was shapely though. With full C cup breasts, a handful of ass, and a washboard stomach, she appealed to many. It was funny how we were similar in that way.

"Hey, love," I greeted and took a sip of Reposado. I'd been posted up at the bar, watching her set. "Do you have another set after this?" I checked my watch, and it was a little after nine, but it felt late as hell.

"No, I was scheduled for an early shift today. I gotta pick DJ up from his grandmother's house." DJ was her two-year-old son whom she shared custody with her looney ass ex.

For the most part, my relationship with Paris was solid, the only issue was her bd and the fact that he existed. I couldn't say that it was an issue that caused strife in our relationship because Paris was mindful of what problems she brought to my attention. She only came to me about the little shit. And rightfully so because I was a fixer of problems. There was no room for going back and forth with me.

If I said something, I meant it. And I'd be quick to make her son fatherless. I wasn't trying to go that route because I loved DJ like he was my own. Hence the reason why I put concessions in place to avoid unnecessary issues. One of those concessions was putting an end to any drop off/pick up with her bd. She'd made his mother's house the primary location for those exchanges.

"Okay, I'll be right here when you ready to slide."

"Okay, baby. Have you checked in on Monk Man today?"

"Yeah, I just spoke to him on the phone before I came in here. Why, wassup?"

"Nothing, just asking. Let me go change, I'll be back out in a few." She winked at me and switched off. Paris made sure to respect Mahogany's rules of us not being affectionate while she was on the clock.

I did too, and not just because I too respected Mahogany's place of business, but I also didn't want anyone to think that Paris was receiving any special treatment. The only time she got that was outside the club. And anything I did for her, she always reciprocated.

"Can I get you anything to eat, Morae?" Taina, the flirty bottle girl, asked with a twinkle in her eye.

"I'm straight, thanks."

She smirked. "Mmhmm. Alright, have a good night."

"You do the same." I spun around on the bar stool and put my hand up to get the bartender's attention.

"Watchu need, Mo?" My favorite bartender, Corbin, came over with a lazy smile on her face. She may have been the only woman who worked at the club that didn't openly flirt with me. She was just cool.

"Can I get a bottle of water, please?"

"Yep, you want a straw?"

"I do, thanks." Handing me my drink and straw, she left me to tend to the other patrons at the bar.

"You ready?" I turned to find Paris dressed in her street clothes. She had on an oversized hoody, tight jeans, and a pair of Rick Owens sneakers. Her long hair was wrapped up in a tight bun. A stark contrast from the video vixen who'd stepped off the stage not long ago.

"Yeah. Here, let me take your bag."

"I got it, babe. Have a good night, Corbin." Corbin gave us both a wave. Paris and I didn't have gender roles when it came to our relationship. We did what worked for us, whatever that may have looked like at the time. We took care of each other. Leaving the club, I tossed her the keys to drive.

She caught them and looked down in her hand, then back up at me. "You sure?"

"Yeah, just be careful. You fuck it up, I'ma have to tap that ass."

She rolled her eyes and walked over to the driver's side. "I know how to drive, and I know how to fight."

"Oh, I know you can drive, speed demon. This my shit though, so you drive how I tell you to. And I'm happy you can fight, baby. I hope for the sake of our relationship that we never have to shake shit up." I winked at her and got in on the passenger side.

I watched as she adjusted her mirrors and locked her seatbelt before putting the car in drive. Glancing over at me, she stuck her tongue out.

"You know you one fine ass bitch, right?" She let out, making me chuckle.

"Yeah, I do." Leaning over, I planted a soft kiss on her lips. "We look good together."

"Mmhmm, less talking more kissing." I smiled and obliged her by parting her lips with my tongue. We engaged in a passionate kiss that made goosebumps rise up on my arms. I felt Paris' hand on my neck and knew what was coming next. No sooner than she broke the kiss to run her tongue down my neck, my phone rang.

"I swear people be doing shit at the wrong time," I fussed and pulled back from her.

She giggled. "It's okay, baby. Take your call and put your seatbelt on."

The only reason I answered was because I saw Money's name on the screen. I was willing to bet that Monk Man had beat me calling him. "Hello," I answered with a hint of irritation in my tone.

"Let me hang up and call again. Hopefully when I call back, my loving, happy sister will be on the other line." And like the fool he was, he ended the call.

"This nigga really irks me sometimes," I said out loud and Paris thought it was the funniest thing.

"Money is jokes," she commented. "Look, he's calling back," she pointed out.

"What, Money?" I answered only for him to hang up again and this time I had to laugh. When the phone rang again, I answered on the first ring.

"You know I can do this shit all day, sis."

"I know and I wish you'd find a woman so you can get on her nerves and not mine."

"Well, you know who I want and until she comes to her senses, it's me, you, and Paris, sis." I shook my head and Paris was just beside herself with chuckles.

"Watchu calling me for, bruh?" I asked, not in the mood to go back and forth about his crush.

"You really got a bad attitude tonight. Paris ain't giving you no pussy or it's that time of the month?"

"Montez, I'ma bout to bang it on you forreal."

"Aight, damn, chill out. Two things, we need to pull up on Trick and the new young bull on his team tomorrow. And I'm gonna pick Monk Man up later tonight."

"Sounds good, that was already my plan. And Monk Man think he slick... he only want you to pick him up cause I said he had to be out by one."

"The party end at two though."

"I know that. I don't want him leaving when the party let out and I don't want him in no shit. You know how shit get, Money. I'd hate for there to be bloodshed if we can avoid it." I was coming all kinds of crazy behind my blood, especially my baby boy.

"I'll get him, Mo. Don't worry about it."

Sighing, I let up. "Aight, is he staying with you tonight?"

"I didn't plan on it, but he can."

"Okay, cool, do that. I love you and be safe."

"Love you more, sis, and getchu some pussy. It does the body good." Having had enough of his shit, I hung up the phone.

"I love y'all bond," Paris said as she strategically whipped my car on the expressway.

"Me too. That nigga is a pain in my ass. I can agree with him on one thing he said though."

"Oh, yeah, what's that?" She stopped at a red light and focused on me.

"Me getting some pussy." I licked my lips and rubbed my hands like Birdman.

"You know I got you, baby." Blowing a kiss at me, she pulled off just as the light turned green. My night was sure to end well.

CHAPTER THREE - TIFFANY

I woke up this morning before my nine o' clock alarm after a well-rested night. After ensuring Mahogany got home safe, I took it in early. I did a thirty-minute workout in my home gym, made myself a smoothie, and watched an episode of Market Mondays on YouTube that I'd missed earlier in the week until I fell asleep. Although the day was a short one yesterday, it was filled with a lot of activity. I was fine with it though.

I wouldn't trade my position at The Table for the world. I loved being a part of the organization alongside my sisters. We were some thoroughbreds who didn't fuck around, and you could tell that we were born to play the positions we played. Sitting up, I cracked my neck and pulled the plush duvet back, revealing my naked body. The only light that could be seen in the dark room was from my ceiling where I'd had my interior designer have the lighting mirror that of the night sky. Swinging my legs around, I put my feet down, allowing them to sink into the mink carpet.

As I went to stand, my phone rang on my nightstand. People knew not to call me before nine unless they were family, so I knew it either had to be Mahogany, Mo, or one of my parents. Reaching over to grab the phone, the screen displayed my dad's name. I answered before it could ring a third time.

"Good morning, dad."

"Grand rising, princess." He greeted me in his signature baritone voice.

"How you feeling?" I questioned while connecting my AirPods in order to move around freely.

"I'm good. I didn't call to hold you up. I wanted to let you know that I won't be able to make brunch today." I stopped pulling at my curtains and repeated his statement to make sure I heard him correctly.

"You're not gonna be able to make it? What's wrong, dad?" My brow raised, trying to figure out what he may have going on that would make him miss our brunch.

It had been our thing for the last two years. We'd eat at his favorite spot and then hit the gun range after. It was one of the many ways that we bonded. He never canceled or altered plans, so I found it rather odd that he'd do it today.

"Nothing to worry your head about, princess. I have something to take care of for Cool. We'll resume brunch next week." Hearing my Godfather Coolie's name, my antennas went up.

"Do you need me?"

"Have I ever? You forgot where you got your skillset from?"

I chuckled lightly and shook my head. "No, and I never will. Well, since our plans are cancelled, I can hop back in the bed until later." Pulling back my floor to ceiling blackout curtains, the sun gave my face a smooth kiss which I embraced.

"So long as you keep with our scheduled range visit, whatever else becomes of your day is on you, princess. Remember, we stay ready..."

"Cause real killers don't have to get ready. And I hear you, dad."

"That's my girl. I love you, princess."

"I love you most, dad. Have a great day and watch your six." We ended the call and I stood at the window with my phone in my hand.

My father was my Godfather, Coolie's right-hand man. They'd known each other since before Mahogany and I were born. Growing up, my father didn't hide what he was into with Coolie and how he provided for our family. In fact, he made sure me and my mother knew our way around different firearms in the event that shit ever went down and he couldn't get to us immediately. We knew how to take them apart, clean them, and put them back together. An ex-Marine, he was a marksman who'd received an honorable discharge after serving his time.

He'd linked up with his old friend, Coolie, that he'd grown up with after being discharged and they'd been locked in ever since. My father took Coolie's sentencing hard and had even planned to take out all those who were involved in framing him, but Coolie told him to fall-back. He let my father know that justice would be served in due time and once he was back home, The Table would still be thriving. And from where I sat, he told no lies. I watched how my father moved with Coolie and emulated that with Mahogany.

It was a good thing that I lived in a gated community, and I was able to stand in front of my window in the nude without worrying about peeping Toms. The homes in my community were yards away in distance. Even so, I probably would get a kick out of someone walking their dog and getting a glimpse of these melons and waxed pussy. Just thinking about it made me giggle. Leaving the window, I grabbed my t-shirt from the couch in my sitting area and pulled it over my head.

Turning on my surround sound system, I let the sounds of the rain forest center me. Beginning my morning stretch, I contorted my body in different positions to achieve the ultimate stretch. After twenty minutes, I muted the sounds and prepared to sit in silence for the next thirty minutes. In this game, so many things came at us on a daily that it was important to hold onto what peace I allowed myself to have. It was another reason why I was mindful about who I allowed in my space. Hence, the reason I'd taken a step back from relationships that weren't platonic with the opposite sex.

I found that it required too much of my focus and emotions. I may have been a killer, but I was soft on the inside, and I loved hard. I prided myself on making sure that the people around me felt that. My last relationship had the potential to drain me had I let it and he'd crossed a line with me that he couldn't come back from. I kind of seen it coming from a mile away, and after two years, I decided to call it quits before I had to watch a mother mourn her son. It was the best decision for the both of us. My phone rang, pulling me from my tranquil space, and I sighed. Leaning over to see who was calling, I answered and put the phone on speaker.

"Hey, am I interrupting your morning ritual?" Mahogany asked when the call connected.

"Good morning, I was just finishing up. Dad had to cancel brunch on me so I'm free now if you need me."

"Actually, I do. Can you come by the house?"

"Yeah, let me hop in the shower and I'll be right over. You gotta come with me to the range today, too. I told dad I would still go."

"I can do that," she agreed.

"Oh, that was easy. I thought I was gonna have to do some more convincing."

"Ha, ha, very funny, sister. I'll see you when you get here."

"Hi, Aunty Tiff." I heard Beautii in the background.

"Hey, my Beautii girl. What you up to?"

"Nothing, reading a book. You coming over?"

I smiled, already knowing what she was going to ask me. "I am."

"Oooh, can I do your make up?"

"Not today, Beautii," Mahogany answered for me, and although I couldn't see Beautii's face, I could hear the disappointment. "We won't be here for long."

"Ahh, man, alright. Next time, Aunty Tiff."

"Of course. I'll be your muse, darling."

She giggled. "Okay." Beautii had a vast vocabulary for her age, so she knew what I meant when I said muse.

"I'll see you when you get here, sis," Mahogany said, returning to the phone.

"Okay." She hung up and I threw my phone on the bed. Stripping out of my t-shirt, I dropped it on the floor and proceeded to the bathroom.

Turning on my thermostatic shower system, I made the water as hot as I could stand it and waited until the shower doors fogged up before getting in. Standing directly under the mounted shower head, the water rained down on my face. I had a hair appointment in a few days so getting my hair wet was the least of my worries. Putting on my exfoliating gloves, I squeezed some of my Olay body wash onto the glove and washed my body. As I ran the glove over my nipple, it stiffened.

I hadn't had dick in a few months, so I wasn't surprised that I was sensitive to the touch. Wanting to further heighten the sensation, I rinsed my body off and put my leg up on the shower bench. Pulling the gloves off, I set them down on the shelf above the shower bench. Using my hands to explore my body, I gave my ample breasts a squeeze and toyed with my nipples. Continuing to do so with my left hand, I let the right travel downward until it reached my wet mound.

"Mmmm," I moaned out loud as I flicked two fingers over my clit in a circular motion. Slowly sliding one finger inside of my pussy, the tightness was apparent the way my finger got sucked in. One finger wouldn't get me where I needed to go, so I added another and my mouth formed an O as I worked them in and out of my pussy at a slow pace.

With a few twists of my fingers, I hit my A-spot and kept at it until I felt my legs start to shake. Knowing what was coming next, I used my thumb and rubbed it over my now swollen clit. My breathing became labored, a sign that I was about to reach my peak. "Ooouu, fuck." Biting on my lip, I feverishly played with my clit and after a few tugs, I climaxed. "Shittttt," I cried out in pure ecstasy. I slowly let my leg down and breathed slowly, basking in the pleasure. I didn't play with myself often, but when I did, this was always the outcome. What a way to start the day.

Arriving at Mahogany's place, I punched in the code to the gate, and the doors opened a few seconds later. Driving up the windy driveway to her house, I parked at the top of the driveway, next to a few of her cars. Now, if my house was considered big, Mahogany's mini mansion was massive. She had the home built from the ground up two years ago and the house was beautiful. Out of the three of us, I would consider Mahogany the most high maintenance.

After her, it was me, and then Mo. And while we all liked nice things and knew how to put that shit on, Hogany was different. Every day was a fashion show for her. Me, on the other hand, I went with the flow and most of the time with the occasion. I didn't know what we'd get into today, so I kept it casual in Milano jeans, a matching turtleneck top, and a Gucci bubble coat to keep me warm in the Fall weather.

On my feet were a pair of field boots. I didn't know where the day would take us, so I kept it comfortable and cute. Getting out of my car, I went to walk up to the door, and it swung open before I could get to it. Beautii stood behind it, all smiles with her mini pitbull, Lola, in her arms.

"Beautii girl." I pulled her in for a hug, pinching her cheeks and kissing her forehead.

"Hey, aunty. I saw you on the security cameras."

"I'm sure you did, inch eye private eye. Where's mommy?"

"In there with Gran." She pointed towards the kitchen.

"Thank you." I rubbed Lola's head and made my way to the kitchen where I heard Hogany talking with her mom.

"And you need to get off my titty. It don't make no sense that I'm here more than I'm at my own house." Hearing my Godmother, Antoinette, I giggled inwardly. She was a spitfire and kept us on our toes. You never knew what she was gonna say out her mouth. Quite similar to my mother and the two of them were close.

"I thought you were cool with watching Beautii here, ma," Hogany said. "If you wanna be in your own home, I get that. I don't have a problem getting a nanny for her."

"Now, you know that's not what I meant."

"Hey, y'all," I announced my presence while entering the kitchen.

"Hey, sis," Hogany greeted, pecking my cheek.

"Hi, Goddy," I spoke to my Godmother, calling her by the nickname I'd given her.

"Shit, tryna talk to this spoiled one here." She pulled me in for a hug.

"Mama, you can go back home, forreal. I ain't trippin'. I wanted you to come here so that you wouldn't have to be home alone with daddy being gone. And I also needed some help with Beautii..."

"Who has a father," Goddy cut her off.

"Who she sees as well. So, what are we really talking about?"

"We talking about you allowing him to slack on his duties because he's in his feelings about some shit he can't change." Mahogany cut her eye at her mother, and I put my hand up to interject.

"I'll be in the den if y'all need me," I announced my exit just as quickly as I entered. Although Mahogany and her mother had a great relationship, they had times when they got into it, and no one wanted to be wrong.

"No stay, you know I'm right Tiffany." Goddy was looking for a cosigner and I wanted no parts.

"Ma, I don't wanna do this now. If you wanna be home, be home. We don't have to beef about it. It's really not that serious."

"Well, it is to me. It's serious to me when my grandbaby comes to me asking questions." Goddy got up and before she left the kitchen, she gave another piece of her mind. "Check that shit, Mahogany. If he can't be a father to his kid in all aspects, then a motherfucka like that don't deserve a seat at The Table. Check it before daddy gets wind of it. You look cute, gangsta." She complimented me and made her exit.

Mahogany watched as she left out and shook her head. "Come on, let's go in the den." Grabbing her phone from the island in the kitchen, she walked out, and I followed behind her.

"What was that about?" I asked, closing the door to the sound-proof room behind me.

"Briscoe has been slacking on his fatherly duties and she's starting to pick up on it. It's pissing her off because she doesn't think I'm doing anything about it."

I took a seat on the white, leather sectional while she headed for the wet bar. I watched as she poured a shot of D'usse in each glass and held one out for me.

"Damn, this early," I said, getting up. Taking the glass from her, I leaned up against the fully stocked bar. Hogany barely drank the hard stuff but had all kinds of liquor stocked.

"Yea. I just need to take the edge off." Her brows creased as she took the shot back.

"So, what are you doing about it? And is he the reason Beautii wanted to have that one on one with you last night?" I tossed my shot back and sat my glass down. "Ughh, water." I held my hand out for a

24

bottle and she handed it to me with a smirk. "Next time, tequila me please."

"Got you. And yes, it's why Beautii wanted to talk. You know she's not the child to say when something is bothering her and for her to bring up his absence to me and now my mom, that's a problem. I've noticed the distance as well and while I've been trying to cut him some slack and carve out more time to be there for Beautii, he's fucking up a good thing."

"Sounds to me that he's fucking up all across the board. Remind me again, why we still allowing him to have a spot?"

"Money, Tiff. You know how that shit moves me."

"Is that really the reason?" I asked skeptically.

"What you mean? What you tryna get at?"

I twirled the glass around on the counter and stared at her. "I know you, Mahogany. It's a reason why you letting that nigga play in yo face. And when you ready to tell me, I'll be ready to hear about it. I'ma go with Goddy on this one, though. That nigga is treading on thin ice."

"I gotta go see my dad's lawyer today, but we gotta make a stop along the way." She avoided what I said by changing the subject and I let her. Picking up the glasses, she put them in the sink behind her.

"We taking your car or mine?"

"Umm, lets take one of mine." She came from around the bar and went to head for the door to leave.

"Hey," I called out to her, "do I have on the right attire?" I looked down at my outfit and back up at her.

"You got yo' twin on you?" She asked, referring to my .45.

"Never leave home without her."

Smiling, she nodded her head. "In that case, you look real good, gangsta. Let's ride." She said all she needed to say without saying much. We were about to get into some kind of action today.

CHAPTER FOUR – MAHOGANY

As I rode in the passenger seat of my car, I sent a text message to Briscoe, letting him know that we needed to get up for a one on one. The moment was long overdue and if I was being honest with myself, it was partly my fault. The last thing I ever saw me having to do was pull his card about him not being about his business when it came to our daughter. Especially when he was the one that begged me to keep her. When I found out I was pregnant with Beautii, the last thing on my mind was being someone's mother.

I was only months away from opening the Elite Palace and constantly on the go. If I wasn't on a plane for a spur of the moment meeting for The Table in place of my dad, I was somewhere handling some type of business. Either way it went, I wasn't ready to halt my movements just yet and be tied down to a child. While I didn't feel ready, we weren't doing much to prevent it. Briscoe didn't want anything to do with any kind of contraceptive and I was okay with that. He was my man, and I was his woman. And he knew not to play with me out in the streets with these nothing ass bitches.

When I showed him the two Clear Blue pregnancy tests, he swept me off my feet and swung me in the air. The happiness that exuded from his body was enough to make me produce a small smile. Although I didn't wanna ruin his moment, I kept it real with him, letting him know that I didn't feel it was the right time. He wasn't trying to hear it. Knowing that he couldn't tell me what to do with my body, he had me list the pros and cons of bearing his child. When the cons didn't match up, he begged for me to at least give it a week before I made my decision.

I obliged him and, in that week, I'd seen Briscoe more than I'd seen him our whole relationship. He came up with little cute gifts to get me to come around to the idea of being a mom, and eventually I did. To this day, it was one of the best decisions I'd made and Beautii was one of my biggest blessings. Now, while I was more than capable of taking care of her on my own, it wasn't what I'd signed up for, so a conversation was evident.

"That's the building on the corner," I said to Tiff as she slowed down the car in front of the George Washington Carver Homes in Manhattan.

I was here to see a man who talked too much. Although it was early, there were a group of people sitting out front of the project building, smoking, and fucking off. My Aston Martin stuck out like a sore thumb on the street, but I was okay with that. I was never gonna be the bitch trying to fit in to appease others, especially when I was born to stand out.

"Oh, yeah, I definitely have on the right attire," Tiff let out as she parked in front of a hydrant. "Did you let Pete know that we were making a visit in his town?"

Pete was the head of Harlem and lower Manhattan. He was cool, very laid back, and usually you saw him before you heard him. Now, had it been for any other reason, I would've given Pete a ring to let him know that I would be on his side, but this matter was personal. If it got out of hand, I was sure to have a conversation with him, only if I deemed it necessary.

"Does a landlord let you know when they're sending pest control to get rid of mice?" I asked, looking out of my tinted windows.

"Yes," she chuckled and so did I.

"Well, I ain't no landlord, but I got some exterminating to do." We opened our doors at the same time and got out. Grabbing my Kelly bag, I put it on my wrist and closed the door behind me.

Like Tiffany, I was dressed down in a pair of jeans and shirt. While she wore sneakers, I chose a pair of Prada platform boots. I was a heel girl through and through. With a cropped velvet Prada down jacket, this was as casual as it got for me. Stepping onto the curb, the group of eyes were on me and Tiff almost immediately. I scanned the crowd of about twelve people, four of whom were women. Seeing who I'd come for, I proceeded to step with Tiffany behind me.

"Excuse me, Young. Can I talk to you for a minute?" I asked politely to the guy who I'd come to see that occupied the green bench amongst the crowd. Of the people that surrounded him, Young appeared to be the toughest. Everyone else just wore a mug, appearing to look tough, including the women. They'd have to do more to convince little ol' me, though.

"Fuck you want with me and who are you?" He spat.

"Whose raising these lil' fuckers?" I asked, glancing back at Tiffany. She shrugged her shoulders. "Yasir Janard Yusef," I called him by his government name, making him sit up. "We can do this the hard way or shit, the hard way because I already see you on your tough guy shit to impress your little friends. As a matter of fact, I don't like the fact that y'all standing around staring, making me look like a spectacle. Clear this shit, Tiff."

POP! POP! POP! Tiffany let off three shots in the air and the crowd scattered. Young looked like he wanted to move, but I assumed by the shock written on his face, he was scared that one of the bullets would be for him next. He was correct.

"All good," Tiffany said, nonchalantly.

"So, tell me Yasir, do you know a man by the name of Coolie?" He quickly shook his head no. "Ain't no way you turn a mute that fast. Do you know a man by the name of Coolie?"

"No," he responded verbally.

"It's funny, he doesn't know of you either but somehow your name was on some paperwork it shouldn't have been on, saying some things you shouldn't have said. I mean, seeing that you don't know the man.

That make sense to you?" I pulled my gun from my purse and his hands quickly shot up.

"I swear man, they told me what to..." POP! I put a bullet in the middle of his forehead, tucked my gun away, and headed back to my car. I didn't like being lied to and had he just kept it real from the start, I could've let him live long enough for a complete interrogation, but he fucked that up.

You see, Young was one of a few people listed on paperwork as a witness to a murder I knew for a fact that my father didn't commit. Young wouldn't have known my father to know what he looked like even if he walked past him, so why he was able to point my father out as the triggerman was crazy. "One down, about five more to go," I said to myself as we pulled off.

Before we could turn the corner, I heard sirens at the same time my phone ring. The police must've been in the area to arrive so quick. Pete's name popped up on my screen and I answered on speaker. "Pete."

"Mahogany, do we need to talk?" He questioned in a calm, respectful tone.

"Do we?" I countered and my phone beeped, indicating another call coming through. "Gimmie a few Pete, I'll hit you back." I disconnected the call and clicked over. "Good morning, Detective," I sang into the phone.

"You on your bullshit early, huh?" The detective on the other end of the phone inquired.

"I'm not sure I follow."

"George Washington Carver."

"Hey," I shrugged my shoulders, "you have your way of keeping the streets safe and I have mine. Either way we're getting it done, right?"

I could hear him sigh on the other end as if I was stressing him. "You're making more work for me, Mahogany."

"And you get paid well to do it. I'd love to chat more but I gotta run and you have work to do. I love you, Dudas."

"Hmph, I'll believe it when you stop doing shit like this."

"I'll do my best, but I can't make any promises, Detective Maurice. You have a good day catching the bad guys." I ended the call and dialed

Pete back. Having one of the city's top homicide detectives on payroll was a plus in so many ways. What made it even better was that he was family. Detective Maurice James aka Dudas was Morae's brother. It paid to be a bitch with connections.

My visit to my father's lawyer's office was a frustrating one to say the least. Like with the last visit, they weren't telling me what I wanted to hear when it came to my father's case. There were no updates or anything, in fact they seemed tight lipped with information. That let me know they were either instructed to do so by my father or they didn't have shit. I hoped it was the latter. My father knew I hated to be left out when it came to his case.

He had told me on the last visit that he wanted me to focus solely on my business and let the lawyers handle his case. That was easier said than done when he and I both knew how I was coming behind him. I wasn't gonna leave his life in the hands of the lawyers again. We paid top dollar, and he was still sent away. With that said, depending on someone else to get my father out of his jam was dead. I was gonna do my part and deal with him later.

"You sure you don't want me to come in with you?" Tiff asked as we parked in front of the printing shop that Briscoe owned with his brother. He hadn't answered the text I'd sent earlier. It was fine by me because he knew that if he didn't come to me, I had no problem finding him.

"No, I'm good. If you wanna take the car back to the house and get yours, I can get a ride back home." She gave me a look that said, yeah right. I chuckled. "I guess you'll be here waiting on me, huh?"

"You guessed right," she confirmed.

"I won't be long," I said, pushing the passenger side door open.

"Wait, you're not taking your bag?"

I thought about it and shook my head no. "I got my phone."

"Mmmhmm." She side eyed me but said nothing and I didn't offer an explanation. Closing the door, I put my hands in my coat pocket and walked into the printing place.

The reason I chose not to bring my bag in was because I knew what I was capable of and with Briscoe being a hothead, things could go left real quick. I wanted to confront him peacefully for the sake of our child. Opening the door, it chimed, signaling my entry.

"Hey, how you... oh shit, what you doing around these parts?" L.A., Briscoe's brother, spoke with his arms outstretched as he walked from the back of the shop towards me.

"Wassup, L.A.?" I held my hand out for him to shake and he laughed.

"Still mean as the last time I seen you, huh."

"I ain't hardly mean. Yo' ass too damn friendly, always have been." Every time I saw L.A., he had his arms out to give me an uninvited hug; shit was weird.

"Man, aight," he waved me off. "Bro in his office back there."

"Thank you," I said politely. I started in that direction when he spoke again.

"How's my niece doing?"

"Still perfect, like her mama. Thanks for asking." Continuing towards the back, I pushed through the double doors and stood in front of a door labeled "office." As I raised my hand to knock, I heard Briscoe's voice.

"It's open."

Twisting the knob, I pushed the door open to enter. Briscoe sat behind a desk, pretending to be busy, which made me laugh inwardly. I helped myself to a seat and got comfortable, crossing one leg over the other. I watched him in silence for a few seconds to get my thoughts together.

"Wassup, everything alright with my baby?" He spoke first, breaking the silence.

"Why do you insist on fucking with me, Bryon?" Hearing his government called, he gave me his undivided attention.

"Man, wassup with my baby? Your text said we needed to have a conversation about her. She good?"

"Don't play in my face, okay. It's no reason you're asking me if our daughter is good when she has every electronic out that you can contact her on. Which is the very reason I'm here."

"To question my parenting? You know we not at one of The Table meetings, right? Act like you know what the fuck going on Hogany."

31

"No nigga, you act like you know what the fuck going on and come correct when it comes to our child or move the fuck around. I've been real patient with you, but you treading that line like a motherfucka. And just like I know you, you know me. Ion know what's been up witchu lately."

"You are what's wrong with a nigga. Ever since you've taken on this new position, shit been going to your head. You letting this shit change you and I never thought I'd see the day."

My face contorted and I sat up in the chair. "Our nine-year-old daughter is starting to think that your lack of attention somehow has something to do with her, and you in here talking about how I run shit? You deadass right now?" I didn't know if I was more annoyed or turned off with his bitching. He was really in his feelings.

"Yo, don't come in here acting like a nigga don't do his part. You know Beautii is my life. Have I been inconsistent lately? Yeah. I'm man enough to admit that. It ain't all me though."

"Are you implying that I'm keeping you from seeing your child?" I was insulted that he would even try to spin this shit on me. His silence said it all. "Look, let's put some shit on the table so that there is no confusion going forward and we don't have to revisit this. I expect more of you as a father because our daughter deserves that and then some. I don't know what you got going on but before I was put in this position, we didn't have these issues."

"You done?" He asked sarcastically, standing up from the chair he sat in. "Cause I got shit to do."

Running my tongue across my teeth, I nodded my head and stood too. "Yeah, I'm done. I respect you Briscoe, but you know it don't take much to lose my respect. Please, for your sake, don't play with our child and her feelings. The last thing I wanna do is cut one of my money makers, but you know Beautii comes before all this shit." I went to turn around and he spoke to my back.

"Damn, yo' rank made you cold enough to threaten the father of your child?"

I glanced over my shoulder and my eyes zeroed in on his. "No, I just made a promise to the nigga who seems more interested in my position than being the father he promised to be. When you tap in with Beautii's dad, you have him give her a call, and not a minute sooner."

Whatever else he had to say after my statement meant nothing to me, so I didn't stick around to hear it. I didn't play about a lot of things and Beautii was at the top of that list. L.A. tried talking to me on my way out, but I ignored him. I heard him call me a bitch under his breath and I chuckled.

"That bitch, L.A.," I made clear, "and don't you ever forget it." Pushing the door open, I headed back out to the car with Tiffany. I hoped that Briscoe took heed to what I said. I wasn't going for no half ass parenting going forward. This was a courtesy call.

CHAPTER FIVE – MORAE

I woke up with Paris under my arm, sleeping peacefully. Her lips were puckered, and I gave them a light peck. She stirred a little and put her hand around my waist to pull me close to her. Paris loved being up under me, hence the reason her leg was wrapped around mine comfortably. Smiling, I looked up at the clock on the wall. It read nine a.m, time for me to get up because I had business to handle with Money. Although I wouldn't mind laying up with Paris for a few hours, I had to ensure the business was taken care of first. I went to move her arm and she tightened her grip on my waist.

"Mmm, where you going?" She questioned with her eyes still closed.

"I'm about to check on DJ then jump in the shower. I have business to take care of." I went to move her arm again and this time she let me.

"I'll get him, baby. You go take your shower." I sat up on the edge of the bed to stretch while she climbed out of it. She wore an oversized t-shirt with nothing underneath it while I slept in my bra and panties. I watched as she slipped on her pajama pants and turned to face me. "Why you watching me?" She smirked.

"Just admiring you." I got up and she licked her lips.

"You like what you see?"

"I do. And if I had the time, I'd lick you from your lips to the back of your ankles." She bit her bottom lip, and I felt my nipples harden. Paris didn't have to do much to turn me on. Just being in her presence heightened all of my senses.

"How you gon' say all that to me and expect me not to wanna do nasty things to you?" Moving towards me, she started to lift her shirt up.

"Maaaa," DJ called out to her, and I cracked a smile.

"Oh, I just know he lying," she huffed while pulling her shirt back down.

"Don't do him like that. Go see what he wants." Pulling her by her chin, I kissed her softly on her lips.

"Mmmm. I love you, Morae." Her statement made me freeze up. "Here I come, baby boy." She pecked my lips once more and left the room, leaving me stuck.

We'd never used those words before, and I didn't think we were even at that point. Me not saying it back in no way meant that I didn't have feelings for her because that was the furthest thing from the truth. My feelings grew deeper each passing day. I didn't wanna hurt her by not reciprocating the emotion, so it was a conversation that we would have at a later date. Grabbing my phone from my nightstand, I sent a text to Money, letting him know to meet me at my house in the next hour. Before I could put the phone back down, it rang with an incoming FaceTime call from Mahogany.

"What's going on, sis?" I answered.

"Hey, Mo. What you up to?"

"Shit, bout to jump in the shower and get in the field with Money. I had Monk Man run a background check on Trick's boy and he came back clean, but you know that's not enough for me."

"Okay. Have you spoken with Trick about your plans?"

"Not yet. I plan to talk to him face to face, though. Just on a respect tip, not because I'm looking for his input on the situation." I put the phone on speaker and headed into the bathroom to run the shower.

"Right. Respect goes a long way. Which reminds me, I gotta give

Pete a call back. I made a lil' noise on his side and I didn't give him a heads up."

"How much noise?" My eyes twinkled because violence, when necessary, gave me a bit of a thrill.

"Enough to make Dudas call and scold me for my behavior."

We both snickered and I shook my head. "What he say?" I sat my phone down on the sink and stripped. Mahogany had seen me naked plenty of times, so she didn't make a big fuss about me undressing in front of her.

"He basically said he sick of me making his job harder. My response was simply that he got paid to take care of business."

"Exactly. If it's one thing he gon' do though, is complain but he gets the job done even though he hates our business."

"Hey, that's all I ask. How was your night?" I thought back to how Paris had my legs touching the headboard last night and my clit thumped at the snapshots that flashed in my head.

"I had a great night, sis. A really great night."

"Mmhmm, I just bet you and Paris did. Maybe I should come see about the other team. It's been a minute since I had my cat licked properly."

"Hogany, please okay. Yo' ass picky as hell. The only person that can put up with you is a male version of you. And when you find him, you gotta let me meet him first."

"Yeah, yeah, I hear you. Keep me posted on your plan today. Oh, and don't forget we meet up with Reynaldo in a few days for the re-up."

"Damn, already?" It felt like we'd just made the trip to Colombia a few weeks ago.

"Yes ma'am. That good shit is moving just like I like it." The excitement in her voice matched the big grin on her face.

"Okay, I'll be ready. I'll hit you later once all is settled."

"Sounds good. Stay safe, Mo."

"You know that." I ended the call and stepped into the shower.

"Can I join you?" Paris entered the bathroom and stood in front of the glass shower door. I nodded my head. Without hesitance, she stripped out of her clothes and stepped in behind me. I handed her my loofah to wash me, and I picked hers up to do the same.

"DJ, okay?" I questioned while squeezing the mango scented body wash onto the loofah.

"Yeah, he just wanted me to know he was up and to turn on the tv for him. I'm gonna make him some breakfast after this."

"Cool. Y'all came at the right time. I just did an Instacart order two days ago and the food survived. You know Monk Man eat like he don't know where his next meal coming from."

She chuckled and washed my body slowly. "Leave my boy alone." As we let the loofahs run over our skin, silence fell over us. It wasn't an awkward silence, but moreso us taking each other in. "Baby."

"Hmmm?" I dipped my body under the shower to rinse off.

"You know when I said I love you, I meant it, right?" We switched places, with her now standing in the front to rinse off.

I thought about my response before speaking. I didn't expect to have to address her statement so soon. "I've never known you to lie about anything, especially to me, so I'm sure you meant it. I'll admit it caught me off guard."

She nodded her head. "I just wanted you to know how I felt. I hope it doesn't scare you away. Shit, saying it out loud scared me. It just made it that more real to me." She chuckled lightly.

"It doesn't scare me. I'm not scared to love or be loved. While I don't want to prematurely say those words now, know that I'm not far from it."

She put her hand on my shoulder and gave me a quick peck on the lips. "I'll take that. Ima get out now because seeing this water drip from your skin is making me moist. I'll have a shake for you when you get out."

And that was one of the reasons I continued to fuck with Paris. Shit was smooth sailing with her. She had a sense of peace that followed her and made her easy to talk to. How could I not fall in love with that when the time was right.

I got a text from Money letting me know that he was out front waiting on me, and Monk Man was on his way up. Knowing how impatient he could be, I finished up the shake Paris had whipped up for me. I kissed DJ's head and slipped my feet into a pair of Chanel sneakers.

"Baby, can you grab my bag for me?" I asked Paris.

"Yeah. You want the one to match your sneakers?"

"Yes, please." As I bent down to tie my shoe, the front door opened, and Monk Man walked in with a pair of shades on his face. He gave me a quick wassup and tried to skate pass me. "Aye," I called out to him just as he got ready to walk pass DJ.

"Hey, Monk Man," Paris spoke, returning with my bag in hand. "Why you got on shades?"

"Same thing I wanna know," I chimed in. "Turn around." He did as I requested, and I motioned for him to take the shades off. By his hesitance, I knew the glasses weren't a shield for a hangover.

He pulled them down and I bit the inside of my cheek. There was a long scratch that ran across the lid of his eye and halfway down the bridge of his nose. It wasn't terrible but deep enough to break the skin and piss me the fuck off.

"It's not that—." I shook my head, causing him to stop speaking. Seeing my face, Paris picked DJ up from the small table he sat at and walked to the back of my condo.

"What happened to your face?" I spoke as calmly as I could even though I was steaming inside.

"Me and Chantel got into it at the party. She had one too many and it got a little out of hand. I'm good, though. I mean, this shit sting like a motherfucka, but I'm good."

"So y'all got into it and this lil' bitch put her hands on you? What happened? As a matter fact, it don't even matter. Give me her address." I put my coat on and the bag Paris had handed me across my body. He stood before me, not saying anything. "Helloooo," I waved my hand in his face, "give me the address."

"Mo, I'm good. I'm not gonna fuck with her no more. You don't have to get involved."

"Monroe, if you didn't want me involved then you should've stayed at Money's crib until it healed. Ain't no way you think I'm letting a bitch put her hands on you slide. Then it got the nerve to be some shit that you can't cover without someone noticing. By the time

I get downstairs into that car, that address better be in our text thread."

"Aight, man," he let out in frustration. "Don't go overboard, Mo."

I stopped at the door with my hand on the doorknob. "I ain't gon' shoot the girl if that's what you mean by overboard. I am gonna do worse than that scratch you have, though." I wasn't about to lie to him. Chantel was getting her ass whooped and that was all there was to it. "The Neosporin is in the bathroom. Clean your face and put some on the cut. I love you."

"Love you, too."

I left the house with plans to cuss Money out when I saw him. Exiting my building, I could hear the bass coming from his car as I crossed the street. The sounds of Keith Sweats' "Make It Last Forever" could be heard and while I wanted to buss a quick two step, I was too in my feelings about Monk Man's face. Reaching his car, I snatched the passenger side door open and got in. He was so busy singing the lyrics to the song that he didn't even acknowledge my presence until I reached over to turn the volume down.

"Damn, Mo, what you got going on?" He questioned, irritated.

"Why you didn't call and tell me what happened to Monroe's face, Montez." I was pissed and it showed all in my body language.

"I already took care of it."

"When?" I questioned, calming myself.

"The moment he got in my car, and I saw his face." He put the car in drive and pulled off. I waited for him to explain just how he handled the situation. "What?"

"Why didn't you call me as soon as you found out Montez?"

"Clearly you only hear what you wanna hear. I just said that 'I took care of it,' Morae. Meaning, there was no need to inform you."

I thought back to Monk Man trying to dumb down what happened and figured he'd told Money not to say anything. "Yo ass be overreacting. And I'm not saying what happened wasn't a big deal, but knowing you, you'd shoot the girl, and it wasn't worth all that."

"So, what you do?" While he was talking about how bad I'd react, he was just as bad as me.

"Paid one of the girls at the party $200 to beat her ass. Shorty did her dirty, too. I started to give her a tip for her service, but I'd already overpaid, so that was that."

"Alright." The action he'd taken made me feel a little better, even though I still wanted to shake the lil' bitch up myself. "This is exactly why I don't want him fucking on these whack ass bitches. I bet she was mad about somebody dancing on him or some stupid shit like that."

"Well, that ain't bout to happen, Mo. He a young, handsome nigga with charisma and that French shit. It starts with a "J" I think."

"Je nais se quois?"

"Yeah, that's it. He get that from me."

"How you gon' have some shit and not even know how to pronounce the name, bro?" I laughed lightly.

"Shidd, so long as the bitches know, that's all that matters, ya heard. On to the business, though. I spoke to Trick last night to pick his brain about the young bull, Rocko."

"What he say?"

"He say the bull cool and make the spot he at money. He just got caught up in some dumb shit. He checked him for it, too."

"Is that supposed to make me feel better about him being on the front line with an open case?" Money knew me better and Trick should've known better.

"Nah, I didn't think it would." To me, Trick's runner was a liability at this time and until he got his case taken care of, I didn't even want him to see the product we provided.

As we drove, I thought about the conversation I had with Mahogany about Maurice. He was the second eldest and we always had a strained relationship. Mainly because I moved how I wanted and didn't feel the need to confer with anyone about it. He, on the other hand, felt that as the eldest boy child, I needed to follow his lead. Things between us became even more shaky when he decided that he wanted to be on the right side of the law at the same time I dedicated myself to The Table. Maurice was promoted to detective at the same time Hogany appointed me as head lieutenant.

The Thompson's didn't do police, so to say that we were all shocked when he made his decision to join the NYPD was an understatement. He was still my brother though, and I loved him in spite of his career choice. We were family at the end of the day and even though he didn't agree with the choices I made or how deep in I was, I knew he'd never have a hand in trying to take me or my girls down. Not only because I was blood but because the money Hogany paid him to ensure we were able to move around freely was way more than his salary.

"You good?" Money asked, glancing over at me.

"Yeah, I just spaced out for a minute. All good, though." I looked down at my phone and saw that Monk Man had texted me. I was sure it was Chantel's address. With Money having handled her the way he saw fit, I made a note to just keep the address for my own records. There was no getting around a meet up with me.

We pulled up to the trap I'd seen Rocko working out of a few days prior, and Money parked directly across the street. It was a high traffic area up on Nereid Ave. in the Bronx. Trick had it moving in an organized fashion, though. I liked that there wasn't a bunch of junkies standing around the place or a whole bunch of motherfuckas standing around outside. Like I'd seen the last time I popped in, there were two guys sitting outside on the porch while the fiends were directed inside to complete their sales. There were never any hand-to-hand sales outside of the house.

"You wanna call him over to the car when we see him?"

"No. This ain't no secret mission, we going inside. Besides, neither one of them is Rocko." I went to open the door and he stopped me.

"Mo, I'm in a good mood today."

"So am I, nigga. Come on and get out the car." He proceeded to get out and walk in front of me as he often did. Money was my number two and if I wasn't out handling business with the girls, he was right by my side.

Although he joked around, my brother was nothing to play with. He could go from warm and inviting to ice fucking cold in a matter of seconds. Letting me know that he was having a good day was his way of telling me that he wanted to avoid bloodshed if we could. My response was simple because shit could go either way with me. For the most part, I let the men run their houses the way they saw fit.

I rarely showed face, so the runners didn't know who I was. Today was one of those occasions where I needed to be on the scene, and I planned on being in and out. Money opened the gate, letting me walk into the yard first.

"Aye, can I help y'all?" The tallest of the two guys out front stood up to approach us. The other guy sat on a folded chair, mugging with his hand tucked in his hoodie.

"Is Rocko inside?" I asked politely. As I said, the runners didn't know my face. When I did my weekly drivebys, I would only watch from afar and when something was off to me, I contacted the lieutenants directly.

"Whose asking?"

I sighed and glanced back at Money. I had little to no patience and all the questioning me shit was sure to get me out of character, especially when I asked my question politely. I went to open my purse while Money spoke.

"Yo, one of y'all lil' niggas go inside and tell Rocko to come out. And before y'all get to protesting..." he paused and I heard his gun cock, "don't." Before either one of them could decide who was going to carry out the request, the door to the house opened and a woman dressed in a pair of leggings, Tazman Uggz, and a hoodie walked out. Her whole look read that she'd come over to fuck.

"Aye, make sure..." The guy behind her went to speak and both him and the female stopped short after surveying the scene. I recognized Rocko's face. I watched him reach for his waist and I drew on him.

"Let's not make a scene. Send your company on her way and let's chat." I could tell the female didn't want no static, so she dismissed herself. I put my gun at my side and allowed her to walk pass me without incident.

"Goddamn, that muhfucka thick as hell, ain't she?" Money gave his assessment as she walked pass.

"Rocko, my name is Mo. You don't know me, but I'm very familiar with you. You had a run in with the boys in blue a week or so ago, yes?' He nodded his head. "Thanks for your honesty. I need you to clear the block until you get that situation settled. It's not up for debate and it's not something you need to go and confirm with Trick about. My word is law. At this time, your suspension is only temporary. I hope that you take this timeout to think about how you move and what you plan to do different going forward. Do we have an understanding?"

"Yeah, but, I---."

"No, there are no buts, Rocko. It's either you understand, or you don't."

He wore a solemn look on his face but nodded his head. "I understand."

"Cool. You can go now."

"I got a pack that I ain't finish."

"Yeah, and that's a you thing. Had you not been fucking off with ol' girl, you may have been able to do that. It'll get taken care of, though. In the meantime, get your affairs in order. You don't have to reach out to Trick either, he'll reach out to you regarding your return." With his head down, he proceeded to walk out of the yard. I then directed my attention to the remaining duo. "Y'all make sure that pack is finished by the end of your shifts, along with whatever you were given individually. The money for his pack is not for you to keep. We work as a team so when you're down a man, you still make sure shit is taking care of. We clear on that?"

"We got it," the tall guy spoke up for them. I nodded my head and turned to walk away. The pop in had gone better than I expected. I took out my phone to text Trick and Mahogany the outcome. Mahogany texted back for me to meet her and Tiffany at the gun range.

"Where to?" Money asked once we were back in the car.

"The gun range to meet the girls." His face lit up and not because he was interested in shooting some shit. He wanted to see his crush. "Sucka for love ass," I clowned as I checked in with Paris.

CHAPTER SIX – TIFFANY

The sounds of my gun going off and the smell of gun smoke gave me an adrenaline rush like no other. I was in my element. With the hearing protection earmuffs on my ears, I aimed the Tec-9 at the paper target and lit that shit up. Once I stopped shooting, I carefully set the gun down and pressed the button to bring the target paper close enough to see the damage.

"Damn, baby, you lit that muhfucka up." I heard a voice from behind me and didn't need to turn around to know who it was.

"Why you sneaking up on me, Money?" I requested a private room for a half hour to get my shit off. While no one else would think of interrupting me, Money thought he was the exception to any rules or boundaries I had for myself.

"My bad, ma. I was admiring you from the window."

"Really? I never took you for the weirdo type." I turned to face him and leaned back on the counter, using my hands for balance.

"Don't insult my character, ma. You know ain't nothing weird about me. You also know how a nigga feel about you, so me admiring you from afar shouldn't come as a surprise."

"Don't start your shit." I turned back around and hung up a new target sheet. When Money came around, I did my best to ignore his sexual innuendos and professions of love for me.

He wasn't subtle about it at all and had been vocal about his feelings for me over the years. Even during my time when I was in a relationship. This man told me I was going through a phase. In fact, he added that any man I dealt with prior to deciding to give myself to him was just a phase. I always took Money seriously and because I did, I tried to keep my distance.

"How you been?" He asked sincerely.

"I'm good. What you need?" I put the earmuffs back on, loaded another magazine into the Tec-9, and hit the button for the machine to center the target sheet.

"You." I expected an answer similar to that.

"I'm unavailable." Aiming at the center of the target, I let the Tec sing. Rat-tat-tat-tat-tat-tat. I didn't stop shooting until the clip was empty. I hit the buzzer on the wall and spoke through the intercom to let one of the workers know I was done.

"You say that shit all the time and as you can see, it does nothing to deter me."

"I don't have nuttin' for you, Money. I've taken a vow of abstinence."

"It look like I'm hard up for pussy, Tiff?" My eyes scanned him as if I'd never seen him before.

Money stood at 6'4, about 240lbs, and he was lean. His whole outward appearance screamed thug. From the way he sagged his Chrome Heart jeans down to the Constructs that adorned his feet. He wore a leather Pelle jacket and a beanie over his waves. I couldn't compare Money to anyone when it came to facial features, he was just Money. Fine as hell, with rich chocolate skin, piercing eyes, and the man had the nerve to have dimples. Overall, he was a catch which was why I kept our interactions short.

"You are... for mine," I countered with a straight face.

He stepped closer to me, invading my space. "You know I'd tear that pussy up if you gave me the chance, right?" The smirk that adorned his face was a sneaky one that I returned.

I leaned in and put my lips to his ear. "I know and truth be told, my pussy could use a good strokin'. I'm just afraid of what I'd do if I found out the next bitch was getting those same privileges." Pulling back from him, I stared in his eyes. "I can't take that chance."

I wasn't one to downplay my feelings or beat around the bush. Being with Money had crossed my mind a time or three, but I knew I'd be crazy to think he was ready to give up his whoreish lifestyle, so it would remain business only between the two of us. I heard the door open and one of the employees at the range peeked in.

"All set?" He asked.

"Yes, thank you." I walked around Money to the door to exit.

"Look at that ass if you want to, playa. I'll let that Tec do its thing and air this bitch out." Money casually threatened the pale face white guy whose face turned red.

"Oh my God, come on boy." I grabbed Money by his arm and pulled him out of the room. "What is wrong with you? That man was not looking at my ass, crazy."

"How you know, you got eyes in the back of your head?"

"You know what..."

"What?"

I snickered. "Nevermind, bring yourself before you get us put outta here. That man looked scared."

"He ain't gotta be scared, but when it comes to you, he sho'nuff better be careful."

"Now why y'all let this man come and interrupt me, knowing he don't know how to act?" I walked to the lobby where Hogany and Mo were waiting with Money right behind me.

"I know how to act. I think I reacted well back there, thank you very much." Money spoke in defense of himself, causing me to shake my head again.

"What he do?" Hogany asked, giggling. "I told him to let you get your shit off in peace."

"In her defense, she did, but you know I got a hard head," he reasoned. Mo said nothing because she knew how her brother cut up behind me.

"He threatened one of the guys that work here."

"Now why you lyin' on me, bae? I ain't threaten him. What I stated was in fact going to happen."

I sighed. "I ain't even gonna go back and forth witchu. Y'all ready?" They both nodded their heads.

"Good, let's go grab lunch, courtesy of this guy." I pointed to Money who shrugged his shoulders.

"You ain't said shit. You actin' like a nigga can't treat y'all to a lil' IhopTM. And it's all you can eat pancake day, let's do it." He slapped his hands together and we all looked at him crazy.

"Nigga, do we look like one of them groupie bitches you like to be seen with?" Mahogany spoke. "You betta act like you know."

"Exactly. You most definitely tried it, bro." Mo added. He took a half step back and covered his mouth with his hand.

"Ooh, y'all gon' act like y'all don't eat Ihop now? Cause we was just there with dad two weeks ago, Mo. Get the fuck outta here."

I spoke for us. "Yeah we do, but not when it's on your dime, playboy. Come on, I know the perfect spot."

We left the gun range, and I watched as Hogany's slick ass slid into the passenger seat of Mo's car while Money got into mine. Leave it to her to be out here trying to play matchmaker. Money beeped my horn and signaled for me to get inside of the car. I had never met a man so bold in all of my life, well, outside of my dad and Coolie. Money had traits similar to the both of them.

"Why you always giving me a hard time, Tiff?"

I started my car and pulled out ahead of Mo and Hogany. "I don't give you a hard time, Money. You give yourself a hard time by continuing to pursue me knowing you're not ready for me. On top of that, we're in the same business so you and I both know that we barely have time to spare."

He scoffed. "How you manage to make time for ol' boy?" I knew he was referring to my ex.

"We weren't in the same field. He was kind of an escape for me." I'd never admitted that out loud before, but it was the truth.

"I guess. How you know a nigga like me can't be your escape?"

His question silenced me because truthfully, Money and escape didn't go together to me. Was he calculating? Yes. A little brash at times? Yes. And a whole lot of gangsta. Escape was nowhere in between those things. "Montez, I..." My ringing phone cut me off. I picked it up from the center console and scanned the caller id. It read unknown, prompting me to sit it back down. It rang again almost immediately.

"You want me to get it?" Money offered with a smirk. Ignoring him, I connected the call and put the phone up to my ear.

"Oh, it's just fuck my life so you can answer yo' phone."

"Shut up. Hello?"

"Tiffany, don't hang up." I recognized Ellis' voice and sucked my teeth.

"Make it quick, Ellis."

"I miss you."

"Ellis, save that silly shit for your baby mother. Clear my line, thanks." I hung up the phone and kept my eyes straight ahead to avoid Money's gaze.

"Aye, you ever told yo' girls why you really left that nigga?" I cut my eyes at him and quickly focused back on the road.

"It's nothing to tell, Money. What's done is done."

"Is it? I figured that would be something you'd want them to know by now. You never know, they could help you through that. Even though I still don't think it's a thing. Them fucking doctors don't know everything, ma."

"How about we just drive in silence?" I suggested. I was close to snapping on him and that wouldn't have been right, seeing as my anger wasn't geared towards him.

"You got it, ma." He turned his head to look out the window while I shook mine. That was another reason I couldn't pursue a relationship with Money. I couldn't give him the most precious thing a woman could give a man, a child. Outside of my mother, he was the only person who knew that and I kind of just blurted out that information in a vulnerable moment.

"Ellis, if you don't leave my shit right now, I'm gonna put a hole in the middle of your forehead." I stood in the middle of my livingroom in a bra and panties with my Beretta pointed at a dumbfounded Ellis. He was frozen, on the other side of the livingroom, closest to the door.

"Tiffany, just hear me out, baby," he pleaded, walking backwards.

"Do you or do you not have a child?" I questioned while slowly inching towards him. My gun was still drawn and I had no plans on lowering it until he was gone.

"I do but let me explain." The clicking sound of my gun off safety silenced him.

"Save it. I'm only gonna tell you one more time to get the fuck out of my crib before I get mad." I was past that point and on the verge of tears. I couldn't let him see me break, though. "Go!" I shouted and he hung his head, leaving my house defeated.

When I heard the door close, I clicked the safety back on the gun and sat down on the couch. Burying my face in my hands, I cried silently. My heart hurt but not more than my pride. Not only had I been cheated on but my man had bore a child with someone else, knowing my history. For the remainder of the day, I stayed planted on the couch, occasionally shedding tears about what had just occurred. After a few hours of ignoring calls, my doorbell rang and I switched my tv to show my security cameras. Seeing Money outside of my front door, I quickly wiped my face of any remnants of tears and went to the door.

"Open up, Tiff. A nigga gotta pee." I snatched the door open and walked back into the livingroom, leaving him to let himself in and close it. "Damn, you look good as hell for somebody that's in mourning."

"What?" I stopped and turned just before sitting back down.

"I'm just saying, it's a whole sad atmosphere. You got it all dark and shit, blinds closed. If someone didn't die, wassup?"

"Why are you here, Money?"

"You weren't answering your phone and we got a move to make." I gave him a confused look and he matched it. "We supposed to do a pickup, remember? Hogany wanted me to be there to watch your back since she went to court for Coolie."

"Shit," I jumped up, "I forgot." Annoyed that I'd let the bullshit with Ellis cloud my head, and business to slip my mind, I headed to my room, and he put his hand up to my stomach to stop me.

"Hold on, talk to me for a minute," he said. Any other time, I would've pushed him off of me, but this time, I stopped. With my head facing opposite of his, I told him about me finding out that Ellis had cheated and fathered a child. I also told him what had occurred just a few hours before he arrived. "Man, fuck that nigga. You ain't losing shit and it ain't yo fault that pussy stepped out on you." The aggravation in his voice was apparent.

I took a step back and he stared at me. Before I could think about what I was going to say, the words spilled from my mouth. "I can't have kids, Montez. I had an accident when I was younger, and the doctor told me flat out that I'd never be able to reproduce." His response was silence, but he never took his eyes off of me. "Give me a few minutes to get dressed and I'll be right out."

I left him standing in the middle of my livingroom with my admission on his mind. After throwing my clothes on, I walked back out front like nothing happened. Money didn't ask any questions and I appreciated it.

That was a few months ago and we hadn't spoken of my imperfection since. I didn't want to expound on it now. He kept silent as we pulled into the parking lot of the brunch spot that I normally attended with my dad. The girls parked next to me, and Money got out and walked over to my side to open my door. I smirked, letting him be the gentleman that he didn't often show.

"Thank you and don't look at my ass." He gave a goofy smile and licked his lips. Money wasn't gonna back down from how he felt about me; that was a fact. As we entered the restaurant, Mo pulled at my arm, making me stop and letting Money and Hogany go ahead.

"Hey," she spoke, "he got it bad girl. Maybe y'all should get together. I think it'll calm him down."

"Naw, bitch, you should know being with me would only make him worse. I ain't no nigga's peace."

"Yeah, y'all are perfect for each other." She chuckled and entered the restaurant. I needed to be Tiffany and Money needed to be Money, but we didn't need to be together.

CHAPTER SEVEN – MAHOGANY

We were scheduled to re-up in two days and while Mo seemed surprised when I told her, I wasn't the least bit shocked that we'd be visiting our supplier so soon. Product was moving rapidly, and I made it my business to ensure that my people had what they needed to keep their blocks operating smoothly. One of the worse things in the game was running into a drought. Just thinking about that shit gave me nightmares.

Before we headed out to Colombia to see our supplier, Reynaldo, I wanted to make sure that things were good on the home front. First thing to get in order was the little spat me and my mother had a few days ago. I didn't like beefing with either of my parents, moreso with my mother. While my dad could easily get over some shit, she could and would drag it to the death. She voiced wanting to be home for the first time since practically moving in to help me with Beautii, and I didn't want her to feel like I was dismissing her. Shit, my mother was a grown ass woman and if at any point she wanted to adjust our arrangement, I had no choice but to respect it.

"Ma, I'm ready," Beautii called out to me before making her appearance at my door.

"Okay, okay, let me check you out." She did a 360 spin in her school uniform and stopped to throw up a peace sign.

Beautii attended a private school at my request and her dad's disdain. He wanted her in public school, but I quickly shut the idea down. Not because I was against public schooling or felt that Beautii was too good for it, but because of who I was. I wasn't in the game on a low level, and neither was her dad for that matter. There was no way I was leaving my baby out in the open for a hater on the come up.

"You not gon' take a pic, ma?" She posed again, this time with her lips poked out.

"Hold on, twin, lemme get my phone." I laughed and picked up my phone from my dresser. Unlocking it, I went to my camera. Switching to portrait mode, the phone rang before I could snap the picture. "Hold on, boo, this your dad." I answered the call from Briscoe on speakerphone.

"Hey, dad," Beautii spoke with a smile.

"Hey, my favorite girl. I didn't expect you to pick up. Shouldn't you be on your way to school?"

"I am, dad. Mommy was about to take a picture of me when you called. If you don't mind making this convo short before my edges start to sweat, I'd appreciate it, pop."

He chuckled. "Just like ya mama. I miss yo' grown self."

"She ain't grown," I interrupted to correct him. "Go put your boots on, Beautii. We'll flick it up before we leave. Oh, and tell Gran you ready."

"Okay. Love you, dad. See you soon?"

He paused before replying. "I'm gonna talk to mommy about that now, princess."

"Okay." She left my room, closing the door behind her.

"What's going on, Briscoe?" I sat my phone down and continued to get myself together.

"I was reaching out to holla at you about the conversation we had."

"Okay, holla." Sliding my earrings in my earlobes and securing them, I leaned back on my dresser, waiting for him to talk.

"Basically, I wanna get back on one accord with our co-parenting.

I've been out of pocket and as a man, I can admit my fuck up. At the end of the day, Beautii is just as much my responsibility as she's yours."

"Apology accepted." I didn't expect to get an actual apology out of him, but this was close to it. "You can make up for it by coming to get her for the next three days if you're not busy. I gotta go out of town. Is this a busy week for you?"

"Kind of, but I can get my princess. What you going out of town for?" He openly pried.

"You wanna pick her up from school tomorrow here or you need me to bring her to you?" I ignored his question. Briscoe didn't have that kind of access to me anymore.

He snickered lowly. "I can get her from school. Don't tell her I'm coming though. I want it to be a surprise."

"Okay, sounds good." I went to hang up and he called my name. "Yes?"

"Ay, you was out in the projects, in Harlem the other day?" There he was again, in my business.

"Briscoe, you got enough business to tend to, don't add mine to your plate."

"Yeah, okay. You betta chill the fuck out on the special appearances. You're in position now, Mahogany, you can't move the same."

"Briscoe, I've always been in position. Thanks for the advice though. All good?"

"Yeah. Lata." I hung up the phone and laughed the conversation off. Briscoe wanted so bad to control how I moved.

"Hey, you driving?" I turned and my mother walked into my room, dressed casually in a pair of jeans and a loose neck sweater.

"Yeah. I wanted to stop and get my car washed after we drop Beautii off to school."

"Okay, daddy called this morning."

"Oh, yeah? Did you tell him we were coming to see him?"

"Nope. But you know your dad, I'm sure he already knows. I'll be downstairs waiting for you." She went to walk away, and I called her back.

"Hey, ma, about the other day—."

"All good, Hogany. I'm not looking for an apology. I know you well enough to know you weren't offering one anyway."

"I mean, it's not my thing, but I'm open to giving you one as soon as I figure out what I'm apologizing about." I was honest in my response. "I'm not tryna keep you cooped up here, ma. I also don't want you to feel that I'm using you to pick up Briscoe's slack. I have that handled."

"I never doubted that, daughter. It was mainly a matter of the timeline. I don't care what the relationship is, family, friend, or foe, never let a nigga play witchu. And you know exactly what I'm talking about."

"What's understood doesn't have to be explained," I assured her.

"My girl," she said with a smile. "Now come on, I don't want Beautii to be late."

We dropped Beautii off and kept on to a nearby carwash. Being that I was out with my mother today, there was no need for me to call Tiffany out. She hated when I made moves without her. It didn't matter to her that I was a big girl and could hold my own very well.

"You getting the platinum wash that gives you the works or the one under that?" My mother read the large sign that displayed the services offered as we entered the carwash.

"This platinum pus—." I stopped and giggled at the look she gave me.

"I am not yo' daddy, Mahogany. You still gotta have a little bit of tact when we together."

I continued to giggle and held my hand up apologetically. "You right, mommy. Dang, even after I gave birth to a whole baby, you still don't want me to be grown." I slowly pulled into the carwash line and felt my car jerk forward as we were hit from behind. The hit both shocked and pissed me the fuck off. "What the fuck!" I yelled out.

I glanced over at my mother who was already unsnapping her seatbelt off and reaching for the door.

"They got me so fucked up," she let out. Somehow, we managed to get out the car at the same time.

I watched as a man stepped out of the driver's side of an Altima that looked like it'd seen better days and a woman who resembled a man stepped out of the passenger side. Wesley Snipes had the nerve to have a mug on her already hard looking face. The guy, on the other hand, seemed to be more concerned with the damage.

"It's just a little ding," he concluded while attempting to shimmy himself in between my car and his as if to shield me from seeing the damage.

"Little ding my ass. If there's so much as a scratch on my shit, I'm gon' know something." I started towards the back of my car and heard she-man suggest to her man that they just leave.

"Y'all ain't going no damn where until we assess the damages," my mother made clear. "While they look into that, how bout you get the insurance info."

"Bi—."

"Aht, aht," I cut off her insult, "wrong time, wrong bitch." I looked over at my mother. "Sorry, ma."

"You good, baby," she assured me. Just a few minutes prior I didn't have tact, but I could let loose when in defense of her. "Cause you know I ain't gon' do too much back and forth."

"Shut up, Rachel," the guy scolded she-man. "Look, it's just a small ding." He pointed to my bumper and I saw the exact opposite.

"You either blind or don't have insurance. Either way, that..." I pointed to the damage, "is a fucking dent in my $90,000 car."

"$90,000!" She-man repeated, in shock. "And you sitting here trying to beef with us over a little ass dent? Girl, spare me. Baby, get in the car and let's go. The rich and famous can afford to get that shit buffed out." She went to get back in the car but the guy stayed planted.

I had a trick for they ass if they thought they were pulling off. I quickly reached behind my back and pulled out my .380. Pointing it at the duo, I stood firm. "You can go head and try to pull off, but I promise you, I'll tear that raggedy ass Altima up with these bullets. Play with it if you want to." It was best that they took heed to my words because the sun's bright light wouldn't stop me from doing what I said. And I didn't give a fuck who was around.

We had a stare down, but nobody dared to move. Me, because I wasn't letting them off without their insurance or an agreement to payment. They didn't move because of the obvious. I was the mad bitch with the gun and the upper hand.

"Hey, what's going on here?" From my side view, I could see a guy making his way over to us. I could make out the uniform shirt with the carwash's logo once he was closer.

"This bitch is crazy," she-man voiced with her hands in the air.

"Sir, watch your mouth before shit really go left out here," my mother forewarned.

I could've warned Wesley that she didn't want those kinds of problems, but if she was feeling froggy who was I to prevent her from the ass whooping she was clearly seeking.

"Miss, I need you to put that gun down or I'm gonna have to have the owner come out and ask you to leave the premises." The employee's plea and subtle warning didn't deter me.

"Go get whoever you gotta get, love. I ain't moving and neither are they." I just knew I looked like a mad woman, but shit, someone was gonna pay for the damage voluntarily or involuntarily.

We didn't have to wait long for the employee to return with back up. He walked out with a guy I presumed was the owner. I took him in as he took slow, intentional steps towards us. It didn't take long for me to pick up on how fine he was. From his low-cut curls to his almond shaped eyes, down to his full lips that showed no trace of a smile. The way he walked let me know he didn't fuck around and he meant business. I appreciated that because my sentiments were the same.

"My name is Justice and this is my place of business. Right now, y'all are causing a scene and I can't have that." After addressing all of us, he cast his eyes directly on me. "Put that away, beautiful, I'm sure we can figure out a way to handle this in a more civilized manner." I couldn't describe his voice; all I know was that it made a tough bitch like me feel good inside.

I cocked my head to the side. "What makes you think this isn't the way I handle things civilly?" I couldn't help but to challenge him.

His lips formed a slight smirk. "How about you oblige me this one time and we handle it in a general civil way?"

"I can do that," I agreed, tucking my gun away, "but they ain't moving until we come to a resolution about my car." I made my intentions clear.

"Respect. Chris, pull their car around back and I'll ride with them."

He gave instructions and took a step towards my backseat. "May I?"

"Wait, hol' up my nigga. How you just gon' tell a nigga to pull my whip around back?" The bad driver argued.

"Exactly," she-man agreed. "Y'all got us fucked up."

Justice turned his head to the duo and rolled his shoulders. "Let's not make this difficult. I'm only trying to help. Trust me, that car can't do shit for me or beautiful here." He pointed at me and I held back my blush. This fine, black businessman was really laying it on thick and I liked it.

"We not do—."

"Aight, come on, man." The guy cut she-man off for the second time, further pissing her off.

"Is it cool if I take quick ride around the block with y'all?" Justice asked us.

"You better walk your lil' fine self around the back, Da'Vinchi," my mother spoke up. I was too tickled because I had been racking my brain trying to figure out who he resembled. My mother had hit the nail on the head. He was a doppelgänger for the guy that played Terry in the "BMF" series.

Justice laughed lightly. "I respect that."

"As if you had any other choice," I countered with a giggle of my own. He nodded his head and I slid into the driver's seat and reversed the same way the beat up Altima had.

I followed the car, keeping my speed to a minimum in order to keep up with Justice.

"Well, ain't that something, we were supposed to be surprising yo daddy and here you are scouting a man to call daddy."

"Mommy!" I yelled out, embarrassed that she had caught on to me eye fucking Justice.

"Girl, you ain't gotta tell me. I'm literally watching you watch him. Let's hurry this up though so I can go see the love of my life."

My parents had been together for 34 years. My mother loved my father fiercely and had put the ride in ride or die. I only hoped to experience that kind of love with someone. As the thought of love crossed my mind, I made eye contact with Justice who nodded his head and turned the corner. Hmph, I'd take it as a sign.

CHAPTER EIGHT – MORAE

"And he wrote a check for the damage?" I asked Hogany after she'd told me and Tiffany about the run in that she had at a car wash days ago.

We were on our way to the airport for our re-up trip to Columbia. As always, Reynaldo made sure that there was a car service to pick us up and deliver us to a private airstrip where we'd board one of his private jets. It was the reason I fucked with him. The man's customer service had always been A-1.

"He wrote a check for the estimated damage," she corrected me. "I won't know how much the actual damage is until we get back on Sunday. I dropped it off to my mechanic, so we'll see."

"Did you get the digits from handsome?" Tiffany questioned, taking a sip from the nasty ass matcha drink she ordered from Starbucks.

"Bitch, who the hell says, 'get the digits'?" Hogany joked. "Yeah, I got his number. For the sole purpose of ensuring that I got the remainder of my money if there's a balance owed."

"Mmhmm," I let out, silently, calling bullshit. Hogany got that number because she was feeling the owner. It was written all over her face and her body language.

I looked out the window just as we pulled up to the airstrip. The car started to slow down before coming to a full stop. At the same time, Hogany's phone rang.

"We made it and we're about to board the plane, Reynaldo." Like clockwork, Reynaldo had started his calls to ensure we passed every checkpoint.

I sent a text to Money to do a check in of my own. I wanted to see how Monk Man was doing. He was not my biggest fan at the moment. I kept my word like I said I would and pulled up on Chantel. I ain't do too much, but a lil' yoke up and a warning of much worse if she so much as spoke my brother's name. Word got back and Monk Man's conversation had been limited with me since then. Paris said I should've let it go but I wasn't tryna hear it. It was the principle.

"Alright y'all, look, I haven't told y'all this yet but—." Hogany paused and nodded for the driver to leave the car. Once he closed the door, she continued. "We're doubling the re-up this go round."

Both me and Tiff made eye contact but didn't say a word at first. I figured the same questions were running through both of our minds, but we wanted to give Hogany the chance to explain the move she decided to make without consulting us.

"Well," Tiffany started to speak, "was your initial plan to tell us when we landed? Or once those extra keys were back on US soil?"

"No, my plan was to tell you now. I would never have y'all go into a deal blindsided, Tiff." From her body language, I could tell she was offended.

"What made you decide that we needed to double the load?" I questioned for my own clarity and used my question to diffuse any unwarranted tension.

"It's simple; we can handle it. Double the product, the less trips we have to make to Columbia. Plus," she smized, "I think it's time we start thinking about expansion, ladies. We'll talk more about it though." She tapped the window twice and the driver opened the door for us to get out.

"You ladies have a safe trip," the driver spoke. "I'll have your bags loaded shortly and you'll be on your way."

We all thanked him and boarded the jet. The inside of the jet had room enough to fit ten people comfortably. Sitting down, I sat my bag next to me and put my feet up. The idea of moving more product had crossed my mind before, even Money had brought it up to me. Now, the thought of expanding was something new.

Hogany had never hinted at it. The thought of us not being successful in the move never crossed my mind. It was the fact that I knew we'd be good at it; great actually. On the other hand, expansion came with more demands, meaning it would require even more commitment. And while I was down for whatever, my decisions didn't just affect me.

"Hey, have you thought about a timeline for this expansion or where you're looking to expand?"

"I was thinking we'd take on one city at a time, starting with Cali. Reynaldo has all the product we need and then some. We can really up this shit."

Hogany had that spark in her eyes. It was that same spark that got my yes when she first asked me to be a part of The Table. I pledged my allegiance then and I didn't see myself turning back now. I knew that it wouldn't be a decision made overnight, though.

"I'm with whateva y'all with so long as we think it through. We got our people here, expanding would require new crews, which means new personalities, and you already know how I am with new people."

"Yep, mean as hell," Tiffany interjected. I turned and flashed her the finger back where she sat, two rows behind me.

"I am not mean, heffa."

"Bitch, yes you are and that's okay. You come from a line of unfriendly motherfuckas. I still love y'all all the same."

"Montez, too?" Hogany slid her slick question in, making me giggle.

"Yeah, Money, too Tiff?" I added.

"Anyway, y'all know I'm rocking if y'all rolling. I'm here for the expansion. When we going to Cali?" She dodged our question just like I knew she would. Me and Hogany knew better. Tiff and my brother had a connection whether she wanted to admit it out loud or not.

"Shit, if y'all on board then we can start planning over the next few weeks. I'm gonna run it by my dad and yours too, Tiff. I wanna get their opinions and use whateva resources they may have."

Both Tiffany and I nodded our heads. "They ain't ready for a trio of solid bitches that know the game to pull up."

"Yeah, well, they can either get on board or get pushed over. Either way, we want it all." Hogany declared.

We all sat back in our seats, and I peered out the window as the jet lifted off the ground to descend into the friendly skies. Yeah, we definitely wanted it all.

"If it isn't the most beautiful trio in the world." Reynaldo walked out of his villa, shirtless, to greet us with outstretched arms.

"Oh my God, where is your wife?" Hogany asked. "I keep telling you to stop greeting us with that bird chest of yours." She laughed while embracing him first. He squeezed her tightly and kissed her head.

"Que, bird chest? This is the body of a Colombian God." He hit his chest and we chuckled. "Adrianna is on vacation this week; Gianna is here to keep me company in her absence." He gave a sheepish smile, and I shook my head.

Reynaldo tickled me. At 42 years old, he didn't look a day over 30. He was a handsome man, in good shape, standing at five foot seven. On his bare chest, a few war wounds he received over the years were on display, but he wasn't ashamed of them. It also didn't stop the women from flocking to him. He had a wife and a girlfriend who got along well. The shit was strange to say the least.

Reynaldo was the man in Colombia, and we saw that firsthand by the way the people treated him like royalty. Although we always conducted business at his private villa that was equipped with a full staff at our every beck and call, he'd taken us on a tour of the slums where he was raised a few times. He felt it was important for us to know where he came from and what it took for him to make his way to the top. He declared that he'd never live in poverty again, so we had to work as a team to ensure we all remained on top. At least that's what he told us. I liked Reynaldo but at the end of the day, the only team I was concerned with was me and my sisters.

"Bay bay, one thing about it and two things fa sho, Gianna gon' get her time," Hogany commented with a laugh. "If I could choose one over the other for you, I'd choose her."

"Shidd, they both betta than me," Tiffany added. "I would be knucking and bucking behind my nigga. Share what, with who?" She turned up her nose and rolled her eyes.

"I keep telling y'all, I have enough love to go around. They don't lack anything. I take care of the both of them well. It works for us."

"Mmhmm. When are you gonna invite us in, sir?" I asked.

"Lo siento, donde estan mis modales, entrar." He apologized for his lack of manners and moved aside for us to enter. "I have the chef whipping up brunch, so you ladies can go head and get freshened up. The butlers will get you settled in and I'll meet you out back where we can talk business, yes?"

"Sounds good," Hogany spoke for all of us.

We all headed towards the back of the massive villa with each of our butlers carrying our bags. Our rooms were located across from one another, giving us quick access to each other should we need it. I loved the peace I felt when we came out to Colombia. It was a beautiful place, one that I wanted to bring Paris to on vacation soon. No sooner than my baby crossed my mind, my phone rang with a call from her. I nodded for the butler to sit my bags in front of the king size canopy bed and nodded that I was good for now.

"Hey, bae," I answered with the phone to my ear. Sitting on the edge of the bed, I kicked my shoes off and sat with my feet tucked under my legs.

"Hey, I was just calling to make sure you landed safely." I detected frustration in her voice. It was a slight hint, but she was doing her best to mask it.

"Yeah, we just got here not too long ago. What's wrong?"

"Nothing, babe. Here, let me help you, son." I heard her say to DJ.

"Don't lie, P. What's wrong with you? I can hear it in your voice."

She sighed heavily. "I'm just frustrated, bae. I don't wanna burden you with petty shit though. Handle your business and come back home to me."

"You are my business, so wassup?"

"Just the same ol' bullshit with DJ's dad. He has a problem with the pickup and drop off schedule. Talkin' bout having his mother's house be the drop off and pick up location takes him out of his way."

"We'll handle it when I get home. Let me speak to DJ."

"It's already handled, baby. That's the meeting spot and there's nothing else to discuss," she said matter factly.

"If that were the case then there wouldn't be any lingering frustration, love. And the last place I want you to be is in your feelings behind that nigga. So, we'll address it together when I get back. Can you put me on Facetime so I can see my boy?" The call clicked and I answered the Facetime. I could see DJ with his face in the iPad. "Wassup, Poppa?"

"Momo!" He called out, excited. "Miss you!"

I laughed at his wide eyes. "I miss you more, Poppa. I'll be home soon. And we going to—." I paused for him to answer.

"The Beez!"

"That's right, Billy Beez. Love you."

"Love you!"

"Alright, bae. Let me get him home and ready for daycare."

"Okay. Can you check in on Monk Man for me?"

"I take it he's still not talking to you." She cocked her head to the side.

"Nope, and that's quite alright. We won't always see eye to eye; it's life."

"I'll check in and talk to him. Be safe."

"Always."

I hung up first and went over to my bag to unpack. It was time to get down to business.

CHAPTER NINE – SANTANA

On The West Coast

"Coast, pack it up, you're out of here!"

I looked up from my bunk where I'd slept for the last two years and smiled big. C.O. Briggs stood at my cell with a hard look on her face and it wasn't because she was mean; not to me anyway. Baby was mad cause a nigga was going home. We had a little thing going for the last year and while I fucked with her to slowly pass the time and ensure I got my packs in, she'd caught feelings along the way.

"That's what the fuck I'm talkin' bout!" I jumped up from the hard ass mat they called a bed and clapped my hands together. A nigga was ready to get the fuck up outta the chain gang.

My parole officer had me violated for a little ass gram of coke and put away to do the remainder of my ten-year sentence that I'd been released early on. When that square face bitch popped up at my crib on that bullshit, it took everything in me not to violate her. I didn't fuck with her from the first day I was assigned to her caseload. What she called playing by the book, I called a bitch taking her job too seriously. Crazy thing was, that lil' ass gram was for recreational use. Had she really done her job, she would've found the keys I'd just copped that were tucked away, underneath the sink in my bathroom. Ol' funky ass, wide back, water buffalo looking ass cracker.

"I don't have all day, Coast, let's go!" Briggs yelled out and I flashed her a look that told her to chill the fuck out. She could be mad all she wanted to, but she'd better pipe the fuck down.

I hadn't told her any lies or sold her any empty promises. That wasn't even in my character. I kept it real from the jump, she was a means to an end. She was a willing participant in the fucking we did, and I still made sure to skim her down when she got my packs through. I would never let a bitch make me feel like I owed her. I knew with me paying her, she couldn't hold shit over my head during my stay had I decided to stop fucking with her.

Grabbing my Bible from underneath the makeshift pillow, I tucked it under my arm and took slow steps to the cell door. I didn't move on anyone's time but my own and that was behind the wall or out in the free world. I put my hands through the slot for her to cuff me and she did, making sure to caress my hand.

"Don't be sad, baby," I spoke with empathy, even though I didn't too much give a fuck. I was going home to my woman, so this was pretty much the end.

"Open up, 24," she called out to the guard in the control tower. I stepped back and this time the sound of the doors opening felt like music to my ears.

"Ahhh, shit, they letting this nigga Coast loose? They gotta let me out!" I heard one of the guys yell from their cell.

I laughed. "Yeah, and y'all niggas still ain't gon' make no bread!" I knew niggas were happy to see me leave. I had my whole dorm sewed up during my bid. I was the nigga with the product and the connect through Briggs. And wasn't shit moving in the dorm unless I cleared it.

I didn't come in this shit planning to be the big dawg; this shit was just in me. I guess you can say it had a lot to do with my upbringing. I'd get to that momentarily. Now that I was on my way out, these peons could breathe easy. I walked down the tier with an extra bop in my step and my head held high. I was on a mission when I touched down, and I had every intention on completing it.

Briggs escorted me over to ID to get my belongings and I sighed at the thought of having to put on that bullshit the state gave you to go home in. A nigga didn't wanna feel like prison coming out of prison. Before I could start complaining, I stopped myself. At the end of the day, I was getting the fuck away from here and that was all a nigga really wanted. Briggs and the officer in ID exchanged a few words, and the woman handed Briggs a clear bag with my stuff.

She handed the bag over to me and nodded for me to walk over to the holding cell to change. Taking off the handcuffs, she followed behind me and stepped back, closing the cell door for me to change. To my surprise, when I opened the sealed bag, there was a neatly folded Polo shirt and a pair of sweatpants inside, along with a pair of Polo boxers and socks. I smirked, thinking about the clothing package my baby, Renee, had sent in for me. Quickly discarding the jumpsuit, I changed into my outside clothes.

As soon as the fabric touched my body, I felt like I was already on the other side. I knocked at the door, indicating I was ready, and Briggs opened the cell for me. She had a small smile on her face and nodded her head at me.

"Looks like I got the right size. Damn, you look good," she said in a low voice so she wouldn't be heard.

I gave her a confused look, but quickly caught on. She had bought the clothes for me. How she was able to pull it off was a mystery I didn't have the time to figure out. I gave her a head nod, signaling my thanks. Falling in step behind her, I noticed her steps had slowed down. I knew she was trying to prolong the hand off to the next C.O. that would walk me outside. That was cool, it wouldn't change the fact that I was out of here.

"Good luck, Coast," she said once we reached the final stretch.

"Preciate that," I responded.

"Hmph, we'll see you back here soon," C.O. Andrews scoffed. What a coincidence that the nigga who wanted Briggs would be the one I'd be taking my final walk with.

I smirked as he opened the door. "You'll see me sooner than you think. When you come home for Sunday dinner, I'll be the nigga leaving out the front of your crib after having fucked the shit out yo' wife." With a laugh, I walked out the door and bopped out of the prison gates and to my ride.

"Yeahhh, nigga. They done let my motherfuckin' dawg out!" My boy, Razor, hopped out of his all-black Impala with a big Kool-aid smile and dapped me up.

"Wassup wit it."

"Shiddd, I'll catch you up on this long ass ride. Let's get the fuck up outta here though. I might fuck around and get to breaking out in hives if I stay in the vicinity of this bitch too long."

I laughed and got into the passenger side of his car, not bothering to give California State Prison one last look before pulling off. When I found out my official release date, I had requested that Razor come and pick me up instead of my girl. I'd been released a day earlier and wanted to surprise her. Razor was like a brother to me; the only nigga I trusted in these streets. We'd been running our operation here in Cali for the last few years. We were both originally from New York and had moved out to Long Beach when we were preteens.

My pops decided that it was his turn to try his hand at the full-time parenting thing. My mom's protested at first but when I learned that my best friend and his family made the move, I gave my mother the sad ass story about me wanting to build a relationship with a nigga I barely knew. I was closer to my step pops but I kept in touch with my pops through letters over the years. After much convincing and the cosigning of my step pops, my mother agreed. I left her behind along with my four-year-old sister and when I touched down in Cali, I went sideways.

My relationship with my pops grew and we bonded over our love for the streets. He was into the gang shit heavy in Long Beach, and one of the men to see when it came to the drugs. I adopted everything he had going on and he encouraged the bullshit, unlike my step pops back in New York. When he and my mother got wind of what I had going on, they were ready to have my ass on the first plane back to the East Coast. Pops wasn't having it though. I remember both parties going at it, in the end allowing me to make the choice of where I wanted to stay. I chose pops because I loved the life that he allowed me to live.

While I lived good in New York due to who my step pops was, he never took notice of my desire to be in the game. And I wanted the cars, money, bitches, and the notoriety. I didn't want it to come from me being his son either. I wanted to get it on my own. As I got older, I saw the difference in who he was and who my pops was. My pops was a nigga with motion and my step pops was the motion. He was a boss and didn't have to touch the work in order for it to be sold. All he had to do was make sure the players were in place and they moved accordingly. I kept that in mind as I grew into my own.

That said, I'd like to think that me and Razor were doing good for ourselves, but I knew we could be doing better. We were in no way operating on a small scale, but we also weren't plugged in like I wanted to be. At the moment, we were working through a middleman who had direct access to our plug that we got our bricks on consignment from. We were eating, and nowhere near starving, but there was a difference between a three-course meal and a five-course meal. I wanted it all plus the fixings, which was why I had plans to tap in with my folks on the East Coast.

"Catch me up on what's been going on out here." I pulled the Bible I had from my property bag, opened it to the last page, and pulled out a pre-rolled blunt.

"Nigga, you ain't bout to smoke that nonsense in my whip. I got some shit for you. Open the glove compartment and grab that sandwich bag." I did as he said and pulled out a quart sized bag. I could see the sack of weed inside but I wasn't prepared for the smell when I opened it.

"Goddamn, what the fuck is that?" The strong aroma immediately permeated the air.

"That's that cloud 9, nigga. I'm talkin' that shit get you so high you feel like you floating. It make yo dick feel two times bigger than it really is too, no homo. It's a special strand my white girl hooked up."

"You talkin' bout that chemist you were fuckin' with a while back? The one that go to ummm..." I snapped my fingers trying to figure out the name of the college she went to.

"USC," he said, helping me out. "Yeah, Ember. She graduated a few months ago. I'm telling you bro... this bitch is a genius. And it's like, every time I throw this big, black dick in her, she come up with some mo' shit. This shit like magic or somethin'. My nut gotta be the secret sauce."

"Nigga, spare me all the extras, especially the dick talk." You could always count on this nigga Razor to do too much. I tossed the bag back inside the inside the glove compartment. I wasn't tryna get that high right now, I just wanted to smoke some regular ass weed.

Laughing, he continued. "My bad. Anyway, that strand she sitting on is a goldmine. And I know you be thinking the weed some small-scale shit but it's an open market, especially out here with all the dispensaries and shit they opening. I ain't tryna leave no money on the table, feel me."

"I hear you and I'll give it some thought. In thc meantime, what's going on with the business we have now?"

For the rest of the ride, he caught me up on our business in the street and even my pops. We agreed before I did my first bid to keep in contact through Razor and Renee if I ever got jammed up. With him being a convicted felon, I thought it best to not have any communication with him that would give them crackers any ammunition to make some shit up. I didn't even converse with him on the phone I had in there. It worked for us. He had taken a back seat to the game and lived life like the OG he was.

Everything sounded good as far as what Razor ran down to me and it seemed that he had held shit together in my absence which I appreciated. I planned to do a check in of my own once I was settled in and got the jail funk off me. After two hours, we pulled up to my three-bedroom, four-bath house in Glendale that I shared with my girl, Renee, and our nine-year old daughter, Asia.

I made sure to keep my family a good distance away from my dealings in Long Beach. I wanted to ensure their safety at all times. My girl was an LPN and we were able to use her good credit and legal income to get the house. Fucking the real estate agent may have pushed us a little bit over the edge but I would never tell her that.

"Aight man, get up out my car so I can prepare to take this long ass drive back to the hood," Razor said.

I grabbed my stuff and got out. "Nigga, you choose to still stay there."

"Yeah, I like to be close to all the action just like your pops. It's too quiet out here for me. Maybe once I settle down and have me a kid, I'll have a reason to move. Until then, I'ma stay planted in the LBC."

"I hear you. Just don't procreate with that white bitch."

"Nah, nigga. I'ma keep fucking her and using her for reparations though. I'ma get my 40 acres and a mule by any means necessary, fuck watcha heard."

I bust out laughing. "You a fool, bro. I'll be in the hood sometime in the afternoon tomorrow to see wassup and check on pops. Oh, and it's a move I wanna make, we'll talk more about it tomorrow. Think expansion."

"Expansion, huh? Fuck you got up yo' sleeve?"

I smirked. "You know I'ma NWP. Nigga wit' a plan. I'll talk to you more about it tomorrow though."

"So long as that plan leads to getting more money you know I'm wit' it. I'm up though." He started his car and drove off.

"Babyyy," Renee exclaimed when she opened the front door. She jumped in my arms and wrapped her legs around my waist. I held her up and used my foot to close the door. "I missed you so much." She held onto my neck tightly while I inhaled her scent.

"I missed you too, baby. Damn, I missed you so much." Renee had been solid since the day I met her, and she had solidified her position in my life by showing how down for me she was.

We'd been together for twelve years off and on but even on our off time, she still stuck by me. I would be first to admit that I didn't always deserve it. Hell, I was sure if she knew half the shit that I'd done, she'd be over my ass. But what she didn't know wouldn't hurt her and any threat to her finding out my indiscretions would be eliminated immediately. She loved me through my unresolved mommy issues and even encouraged the restoring of my relationship with my mother that was still rocky till' this day. She was a rider.

"I didn't know you'd be here early. I gotta run out and pick Asia up from school, she had a half day. You wanna come? I know she's gonna lose it when she sees you."

I kissed her lips, and she slid down off me. "You go and I'm gonna wash this jail scent off me. I gotta make a call too. I'll see y'all when y'all get back."

"Okay, no problem. Let me hurry up. You want anything while I'm out?" I stood back and took her in. Renee stood at 5'7 with a slender build. She had small b-cup titties and a little more than a handful of ass. She had a little pudge that she'd been struggling with since we had Asia, but I loved it. To add to her look, she rocked a short haircut similar to the one Nia Long had in "The Best Man" and it framed her face well.

Watching her bend over and grab her purse from the couch, my dick rose to attention and saw it as an invitation to get closer. I'd fucked C.O. Briggs two days ago so while I wasn't feenin' for pussy, just thinking about the way Renee touched her toes when I dug in her shit from the back made me wanna do things. Walking up on her, I gripped her waist with one hand and used the other to grab a handful of pussy through her jeans.

"Hurry up and get back here so I can fill you up." I licked her neck and she let out a soft moan.

Sucking in a breath, she pushed her ass into me. "I will, Daddy." I gave her ass a slap and let her go.

"Mmhmm, hurry up girl."

Giggling, she made her way out the door. I watched from the window as she got in her car and drove off. Cracking my neck, I took a deep breath and headed towards the kitchen to make a call.

I mentioned expansion to Razor but the honest truth was, I wanted to relocate back to my hometown on the East coast. I didn't want to make the move blindly though and I damn sure wasn't tryna start from the bottom once I got there. This call would put me in the right direction. I dialed one of the few numbers I had committed to memory and listened as the phone rang. By the time it got to the fourth ring, the call connected.

"State your business," the man on the other end of the phone spoke in a serious tone.

"It's Santana."

"I know who it is, state your business." I'd never known Dorian to be welcoming or friendly with niggas, so I took no offense to his tone.

"I need to speak with the man."

"Is it worth a phone conversation?"

"So long as I'm still family, then yeah." This nigga was too serious for his own good. "Plus, I just got out of the chain gang so I know how he'd feel about a face to face at the moment." It had been a few years, so I hoped that it was still all love.

"I know that, too," he said, matter factly. "I wanted to make sure you weren't on no bullshit. Hold the line." I shook my head and stayed on the line as he requested.

I wasn't surprised that he knew that I was out or that he even knew who I was when I called. D was thorough like that. Hence the reason why he was the right-hand man to one of the most respected bosses on the East coast.

"Young Boss, it's been a while. What can I do for you?"

"Man, I don't know how you manage to still sound cool after all these years."

"Can't give you the secret until you get some mo' age on you, youngin'."

I chuckled. "I hear you. I wanted to chop it up with you about property in your city and maybe a few builders." I spoke in code, letting him know that I wanted to set up shop in New York and needed a few men on my team. The phone went silent for a few seconds which let me know he was processing my request.

"When's the last time you spoke to your mom?"

I sighed and answered truthfully. "It's been a minute. How is she?"

"Her number ain't changed. Handle that sooner than later."

"I hear you. About the property though." He wasn't telling me to do anything I didn't already plan on doing. I knew I had some making up to do.

"I can point you in the right direction. I don't know if you heard or not, but I'm in timeout right now."

"You bullshittin' me," I let out, in genuine shock at what he'd said.

"Nah, it's very much real. I won't be down for long though. Like I said, I can point you in the right direction."

"Wait, so you saying you ain't the nigga to see no mo'?"

"D," he called out to his right hand, "is that what you heard me say?"

"Nah, nowhere close to it," D answered.

"So, you tryna make a move or not?" I didn't like the tone behind his questioning. It came out like I was some bumass nigga that was tryna get put on. And I was far from that.

"Man, all I need you to do is point me to the nigga in charge and I'll take care of the rest." The saltiness could be heard in my tone and I was silently kicking my ass for letting it seep through. I didn't want them to know I was offended. I learned early on that the old heads often deemed the youngins soft when they took offense to shit they considered small.

"Get out yo' feelings, ain't no money in there. Business is still in the family, Santana. It's in very capable hands, too."

Now, I was taken back. This nigga done put some random ass family member in position, knowing I was alive and well. I held in my anger, took a deep breath, and asked who the person was.

"Your sister, Mahogany."

CHAPTER TEN – TIFFANY

♫S trip clubs and dolla bills, still got my money. Patron shot can I get a refill, I still got my money. Strippers goin' up and down that pole, and I still got my money. Four o' clock and we ain't going home, 'cause I still got my money.♫

Rihanna's "Pour It Up" played throughout Elite Palace and I sang the song word for word as if it were my own. It was the first weekend we had taken off in a while and we wanted to let our hair down in celebration of our upcoming expansion. After getting her dad's blessing, along with a few encouraging words from my dad, Hogany was ready to put plans in motion for the takeover.

The Colombia trip had given us clear minds to plan everything to a T and in the next week or so, we'd start execution. For now, we were going to turn up before locking in on our new venture.

"Aye, that bitch said, money make the world go round, bands make your girl go down." Hogany recited the lyrics while standing on the couch in our private section. She had her money gun shooting bills in the air and I got a kick out of it.

My girl was really having a time and I loved to see it. See, we rarely partied in the club because we always felt we had to have our guard up, even now. It was that way 24/7 and it mainly had to do with us wanting to appear as put together as the men in our line of work. Whether we cared to admit it or not, as women in the game, we had to be a step ahead of the men and even more mindful of the way we moved. Although I was Hogany's head of security, there were always people in place watching our back as well.

"Yeah, shake that shit," Mo encouraged through a laugh. She too was lit and we didn't have to pressure her to get there. "Rihanna did her thing with this one."

"And did," I concurred, popping my hips.

"Yeahhh, it's your boy, DJ Ro on the ones and twos here at the hottest club in NY. Shoutout to the boss lady herself, Mahogany! This one is for you, mama." He changed the record from Rihanna to Eve's "Who's That Girl".

When Mahogany bussed out with the Harlem shake, I lost it. Here my girl was, in a pair of Manolo's, shaking her shoulders like she was a part of Litefeet Nation. I couldn't help but to cheer her on through my giggles. "Get that shit, sis!"

She hit a couple more moves, let the money gun off, making the crowd below go crazy before stepping down off the couch.

"I'm having such a good time!" She yelled out over the music.

"I can tell," I yelled back. "It was the Harlem Shake fa' me." I handed her a water and she twisted the cap off, put it to her lips, and took a couple sips.

"I had to let you know I still had it. I saw you recording too, Mo. You ain't slick."

Mo looked up from her phone and snickered. "I couldn't help it, sis. I needed this evidence for when I bring it up at a later date. Look." She held her phone up for us to see and we all laughed.

"You know what, you can keep that. Y'all saw how I dusted my shoulder." She did the move again, making us holler. "Ooh don't look now Tiff, but yo man on his way up. He prolly saw you popping that ass and bout to check you about it." She snickered and I sucked my teeth.

"Money can't check me, I'm a grown ass woman," I retorted. Butterflies filled my stomach knowing he was near and I hated that.

"Oh, so that is your man," she said with her head cocked to the side.

"Girl, shut up and drink your water." I waved her off and turned right into Money's arms.

"Hey, sexy," he spoke with a smile so infectious and genuine, I smiled too. "You're right where you supposed to be, huh?" He used me being close to him as an opportunity to wrap his hands around my waist and pull me closer so that our lips were only inches from touching.

Feeling the effects of the 1942, I put my hand behind his head and my lips to his ear. "You want this pussy bad, huh?"

"Just as bad as you want this dick," he whispered and licked my ear. My nipples hardened against the thin fabric of my Mugler top. "Come dance with me," he said.

"I never took you for the dancing type."

"I'm not. Ima just grip your waist while you throw that heavy motherfucka in a circle."

"Well, damn Hogany, I guess we're invisible." I heard Mo say.

"I know right," Mahogany agreed.

Stepping back from Money, I put my head down to hide the fact that I was blushing. I had no damn business blushing over this man.

"Y'all know I ain't on it like that, wassup Beyonce and Michelle." He went to hug them and neither budged.

"Hol' on now, nigga, which one of us is Michelle?" Mahogany said, making him laugh.

"Yeah, cause what you tryna say?" Mo added with a neck roll.

"Umm, you might wanna come on before you get hurt over here." I pulled him by his arm.

"Yeah, getcho man before we jump his ass. Talkin' bout some Beyonce and Michelle." Mo shook her head and sipped her drink.

I could hear Mahogany tell Mo she was definitely Beyonce and Mo give her a bitch please. I giggled as we walked down the steps, with Money leading the way, my hand in his. As we got to the last step, I could see one of the club's bouncers who doubled as security, Scooter, walking in our direction with a man and woman behind him. I stopped short of walking and pulled at Money's hand for him to do the same.

"Wassup, Scooter?" I spoke to him, but my eyes were on his company.

The guy had skin the color of copper and wore his hair in four braids to the back similar to Nipsey Hussle's. He had eyes that looked like he was in deep thought. His face was vaguely familiar. In fact, he resembled Mahogany around the eyes. The female who seemed to be attached to him stared in my direction, her eyes lingering on Money's longer than mine.

"This guy—."

"I got it, bruh," the guy interrupted before Scooter could finish. "I'm looking for Mahogany.

"For?" Money spoke, pulling me closer to him.

"I'll tell her once I get to her."

"Well, nobody gets to her until they speak to me. So, lets chat, shall we?" I could tell by the way his lip curled up, he wanted to debate what I had to say, but he either went through me or got the fuck on. It was just that simple.

"I'm on y'all turf so I'll respect that." He was trying to save face as if he had a choice, just like a man.

"Cool. Scooter, can you take—."

"Coast," he said his name.

"Can you take Coast and his lady over to private booth eight?"

"No disrespect," Coast spoke, and I knew whatever he was set to say next, I more than likely would take as disrespect, "you can just point me in the direction of the booth and I can walk myself there. I'm a grown ass man and don't need an escort."

"Okay." I pointed in the direction of the booth and he nodded and walked off hand in hand with the female.

"You seen that nigga before?" Money asked me once Coast was out of ear shot.

"Never."

"I don't like that nigga."

"Yeah, I'm on the fence, too. We gotta put a pause on that dance, though. You got your phone on you?" He pulled out his iPhone and handed it to me.

"111891," he rattled off the passcode while he kept his eyes in the direction of where I'd sent Coast.

"Why is my birthday the passcode to your phone, Montez?"

"It's an important day to me." There was no hesitation in his answer, and I took note of it, smiling inwardly.

Unlocking the phone, I dialed Hogany's number.

"I watched the exchange and I'm watching you now. Wassup?" She said when she answered.

"Some dude name, Coast. He wants to talk to you. I told him he had to talk to me first."

"And that's what it is. Let me know if it's even worth a conversation when you're done."

"Will do." I ended the call and handed the phone back to Money. "Let me go see what he's talking about."

"Aight, let's go." He stepped aside, allowing me to walk ahead of him.

Making our way over to the table, the couple were enthralled in a conversation that they abruptly stopped once we got closer. That was the first official red flag that I stored in my memory bank. Taking a seat across from them, Money stood behind my chair.

"So, Coast, how can I help you?"

"I'm here to speak to Mahogany."

"Yes, you made that clear a few minutes ago. What is it that you need to speak with her about?"

"I'm here on a referral about business."

"Business, huh? Are you scouting talent?"

"What you mean?" He questioned, confused.

"Well, you said you're here on a referral about business. This club is Mahogany's place of business."

His eyes scanned the club as if he hadn't looked around when he first arrived before they landed back on me. "Yeah, I'm in a different line of business... sales."

I nodded my head and reached over my shoulder to tap Money. He got the hint and stepped aside for me to push my chair back and stand up. "I'm not sure what sales you're referring to and I'm sorry that the person who referred you wasted your time. Have a bottle of your choice and I'll let the bar know it's covered." Turning on my heels, I went to make a step and his words stopped me.

"Preciate your time. Tell my sister that her brother, Santana, is in town for a few days. I'll be visiting mommy tomorrow."

It was a good thing he didn't see the shock written on my face due to the position of my head. Declining to respond, I kept it pushing. Her brother? Mahogany don't have no damn siblings, I thought to myself. Or did she?

CHAPTER ELEVEN – MAHOGANY

I watched the exchange between Tiff and the unknown man and scanned my mental rolodex trying to figure out who he was and if we'd ever crossed paths before. Nothing about him stuck out from afar, but I figured if he came here and asked for me, he knew of me from someone. I was popular in the club circuit because of how big Elite Palace was and as far as The Table went, people didn't know much about me until they had to see me. I preferred it that way.

Tiffany stood up from where she sat and went to walk away when whatever the man said next made her pause. She looked up and we locked eyes briefly. Breaking the stare first, she continued through the crowd with Money behind her.

"Everything good?" Mo asked, coming up on my side.

"Not sure yet. We'll find out once Tiff gets back up here, though." Stepping back from the balcony, I went to sit back down. My phone rang on the table, and I picked it up to check the caller ID. It read, "carwash." I smirked before answering it.

"Hello, Justice."

"I like the way you say my name." I crossed my legs and sat back in the seat. His voice was so sexy, one I'd come to love to hear over the past few days.

Once we got back from Colombia, my car was ready to be picked up as promised and the damage was way under the $5000 check Justice had written. I paid what I owed to my mechanic and personally delivered what was left over to Justice, in cash at his carwash. The shocked but pleased look on his face let me know that he'd never fucked with a solid bitch before. I was as solid as they came and there was no way I was gonna stiff him on his money when he didn't have to offer to pay in the first place. After paying him, he invited me to lunch, an invitation that I surprisingly accepted.

We went to an Italian restaurant not too far from the carwash, where we enjoyed pasta carbonara, wine, and good conversation. The fact that he could hold a conversation was a plus for me. We didn't have a deep conversation, mostly surface but still interesting. It was enough to where I would be open to a second meet up.

"I just bet you do. To what do I owe the pleasure of this conversation at this hour?" I looked down at my Rolex and it was only 11pm. Still, it was late.

"Honestly, I wanted to hear your voice. Sounds like you're out, though. I can hit you back tomorrow."

"I appreciate your courtesy. I am out now, at my club with my girls. What are you up to?"

"It's a quiet night for me. I had a long week."

"I hear you. Would you like some company?" My thoughts slipped through my lips and my eyes got wide. Okay, I done had one too many, I thought to myself.

"I would, but not at my crib. Nothing against you, but I come from a certain lifestyle and I'm gonna have to know you a little better before I give you such access."

I nodded my head in both understanding and respect. "A cautious man, I like that."

"Not cautious, mama, mindful. There's a difference."

"This is true," I agreed and looked up to see Tiffany and Money coming up the steps. "Hey, what do you think about meeting me here at my club? I know you said it was a quiet night for you, but if you're interested in good music, good food, and strippers, this is the place to be."

"I'll pass on the strippers, but I'll take you up on the food and music. Text me the address and I'll be there shortly."

"Done. I'll see you when you get here." I cleared the line and focused on Tiffany whose lips were in a straight line, letting me know that she was thinking hard about something. Whenever she was trying to figure something out, she had this tight look on her face. "So?"

"He said that he's here about some business. He was referred to you by someone."

"Business, huh?"

"Yeah. He also said that he's your brother," she added. Now it was my turn to have the tight face.

"Her what?" Morae questioned before I could.

"Yeah, the shit threw me for a loop too," Tiffany continued.

"Well, we all know that I'm an only child so he gotta be on bullshit. Did he say who referred him?" I asked, getting up again and going back over to the balcony.

"Nope."

I looked down on the first level and as if he could feel my eyes on him, the mystery guy peered up at me. He raised a bottle of a brand of liquor I couldn't make out in the distance and gestured as if he were toasting to me. Who is this nigga? I questioned to myself.

"What's his name?" I heard Mo inquire.

"Said his name was Santana," Money answered. "Not that you asked, but I don't like the nigga vibe at all."

I turned to lean against the plexiglass and gave Money my full attention. "Talk to me, bro."

"I can't quite put my finger on it. I just know something is off."

I nodded. "I'll keep that in mind. For now, Tiff give Mo a full description of homeboy and Mo you give it to Monk Man, along with the name and see what he comes up with."

"Got you," Mo assured.

"You not gonna go down there?" Money questioned.

"Nah, I move on my time. I'll find him when I'm ready." Turning slightly, I could see the Santana person and the woman he was with get up from the table, clasp hands, and walk towards the exit. "Plus, I have a visitor coming to check me in a few. I'm not doing business tonight, especially in my club."

"A visitor, huh." Tiffany picked up on the tail end of my statement.

"Yes. Mo, give me a few, and I'll have a license plate for you once I run the security cameras. It would've caught him coming in and going out. I'll be in my office if y'all need me." Picking up my phone and my water, I went to head out of the VIP area.

"Uh, huh, bitch you is not slick," Tiffany let me know. "It's been a week and we still don't even know that nigga's name."

I smiled at her overprotectiveness. "His name is Justice, mom."

"Yeah, I'll be that. Mo, go head and put in a background check for Mr. Justice, too." I could've shut the check down, but it was better to be on the safe side, so I let Tiffany make the call. She would've found a way to go around me to get it done anyway. "We'll be here when you're done."

"Sounds good." With that, I took the steps downstairs and ducked off in the back where my office was located. Putting in an order for a variety of appetizers, I sat down in my office chair and awaited Justice's arrival.

Carwash: I'm outside, beautiful.

I read a text from Justice and responded back that I'd be right out to get him. Standing, I checked myself out in the floor length mirror that was in the corner of my office and nodded my head in approval. For the night out I chose to keep it sexy in a Jean Paul Gautier bustier top, Kasia Kucharska leggings, and Manolo Blahnik Hangisi shoes. The all black definitely exuded sex. I ran my hands down my stomach and turned to check my ass. Even in a size 12 with a little bit of belly, you better believe I was killing shit. Sometimes I had to slap my own ass.

Pleased with my look, I grabbed my phone, my baby Ruger from my top draw, and tucked it in the back of my leggings. The club was packed, and I mentally calculated the money I was sure to rake in for tonight. Bad Ass Bri and Cherokee were set to close out the night with their duo performance and I just knew the niggas in attendance were gonna go crazy. Two thick round asses bouncing across the stage, sliding up and down the pole with ease; it was surely a show to remember. Hell, I'd even taken a lesson or two from them that I put to the test in my own bedroom. And let's just say, it was the reason Briscoe was still secretly on my body.

"Wassup, Mahogany, you need anything?" Scooter, the security guard, asked me.

"No, thanks. I have a guest and I'm headed out front to get him." I went to walk pass him and doubled back. "On second thought, come here for a second." He came closer to me, and I gestured for him to bend down so that I could talk directly in his ear. Scooter was tall as hell and had an intimidating stature. The mug he often wore gave every bit of, don't fuck with me. "Did the guy that was looking for me say anything other than he wanted to speak to me?"

"Nah."

"Okay, cool. Keep your eyes open, Scooter."

"Always. As a matter of fact, I'm gonna walk with you out front to get your guest." He put his hand out for me to walk first and I did.

When I made it outside, I could see Justice standing in front of his blacked-out Maserati. The Matte black rims on that hoe were so pretty. Ughh, it was something bout a black man in a luxury car that owned that shit. And although there were people outside of the club, all I saw was him. Not only did the car stick out to me but his casual attire did too. He wore a sweatsuit and the latest pair of Jordan 1s. I loved the peacoat that he rocked to complete the look. I could tell that he was the type of man that did what he wanted to do. Anyone else would've come dressed for the club. Justice came dressed to simply hangout with me.

"Hey, you," I called out to him, and he looked up. I motioned for Scooter to stay back and met Justice as he walked towards me.

"Wassup, mama? I've heard about this place a few times. I would've never guessed that you were the woman behind it all," he said, pulling me in for a hug.

"Oh yeah? I'm the woman behind a lot of things. Rarely seen but always felt." I winked at him, and he smirked.

"Heard you."

"Come on, I ordered a few appetizers off the menu for us. I figured you can order whatever drink you want once you see what we have."

"Cool, I—." Rat-tat-tat-tat-tat. The sound of gunshots cut his sentence off and he flung me to the ground, shielding my body with his.

There was pandemonium outside as shots rang out, and from the sounds, I could tell there were different guns going off. Never one to be a sitting duck, I used all the strength I had to push Justice off me and pulled my gun, shooting at the unknown assailants as the car whizzed past us.

"Mahogany!" Tiffany yelled out, rushing over to me with her gun in hand and Mo on her heels. "What the fuck just happened?"

"I don't fucking know!" I yelled out, pissed that I'd been caught slipping. She helped me up and I felt a stinging in the back of my head and on my back. I knew that I was injured, but with my adrenaline racing, it was the least of my concerns. Twisting my body slightly, I looked down at Justice who was cradling his side and noticed a red circle developing on the outside of his coat. "Shit, Justice! Money, Scooter, come help me get him inside." Scooter tucked his gun away and came right over along with Money.

"I'm good," Justice let out through gritted teeth as he tried to get up from the ground.

I didn't respond, only nodded my head towards Money and Scooter to help him up and we all rushed back inside the club. The partygoers were frantic and scattered quickly, trying to figure out what to do and where to go. As we passed one of the bouncers helping clear out the place, I whispered for him to shut everything down and make sure everyone got out of the club safely.

"We're going to my office," I instructed, and we all headed that way. "Lay him on the couch. Mo grab Bri for me and have her come check him out, please." I took my shoes off and began to pace the floor, holding my head while talking to myself. "Whoever did this shit is fucking dead and that's on everything I love!"

"I'm good, y'all— arghh shit. The bullet went through and through." Justice was doing his best to convince us that he was good, but that shit went in one ear and out the other.

"This shit ain't no coincidence and once we get him patched up, we getting in the field," Tiffany spoke, calmly, although she was anything but that. It was the type of calm that let you know shit was gonna get ugly.

I glanced at Justice whose jaw flexed and he stared directly at me. His stare spoke volumes and I knew he was seeking answers for what had transpired. I didn't blame him at all. Had I been in his shoes, I'd be feeling the same, only I would've been more vocal about it.

"Scooter, go outside and get some order in my parking lot. Too many motherfuckas running around causing an even bigger scene than it needs to be. I'm gonna run these cameras and see how all this shit went down. Let me know when the boys get here cause I'm sure they're on their way." I was seething and I wanted blood.

As Scooter went to walk out, the door opened, and Mo entered with Bri behind her. In Bri's hand was her first aid kit in the form of a medical bag. I'd gifted it to her for her 25th birthday. The contents it held were more exclusive than your average band aid, gauze, and Neosporin. Bri was a RN by day and a seductress by night. She didn't have to work at the club, she chose to because she loved it. When I found out what she did for a living and how she was more skilled than the average RN, she became our go to for quick medical fixes, such as this one.

Dressed in a fishnet one piece that showed her caramel areolas and freshly waxed pussy, she made her way over to Justice. "Okay, let's do this," she said and sat her bag on the floor while kneeling down next to him.

"I'm good, shor—." He stopped mid-sentence, taking in Bri's attire. "Y'all deadass right now?" His eyes shifted from me back to Bri.

"She's certified and this is her lane. Let her treat you and disregard her treats." Shaking his head, he laid back and Bri snickered before going to work.

"I'd be distracted too, bruh," Money commented, causing Tiff to shoot him a look that made him throw his hands up and stand down. "My bad, bae."

"Do you have something in there for her back?" Tiff asked.

"And her head," Mo added, cutting her eye at me. They must've caught me wince as I sat down at my desk.

Bri went in her bag, pulled out a few items, and handed them over to Mo. Mo then sat the items on my desk and entered my private bathroom. Returning, she stood behind me and I heard her mumble something inaudible under hear breath. Whatever it was, it made Tiff's jaw flex. Seeing their reactions, I decided not to react to the pain I felt, although it stung like hell as she dabbed at my shoulder to clean the wound.

Instead, I focused on pulling up the security feed in order to pinpoint exactly where all hell broke loose. I could've pulled the projector down to view the footage but I wanted to keep everything contained, especially with Justice present. Yes, he shielded me from bullets I was almost certain were meant for me but there was no way I'd repay him by letting him in on my business.

"Ssss," I let out and gritted my teeth.

"You, okay?" Tiff questioned.

"Yeah," I lied. "Come look at this." She came around my desk and I pulled the footage that covered the parking lot. It showed me and Scooter exiting the club and me stopping when I noticed Justice. Nothing looked suspicious or out of the ordinary to me.

"Zoom in a little," she prompted. "Pull up the camera on the left side." I did and picked up on a dark colored Acura in the cut.

The headlights weren't on, indicating the car was turned off and that the patrons inside were probably lying in wait. As me and Justice pulled back from embracing each other, the headlights on the Acura came alive. In seconds, I could see a hooded figure lean out of the passenger side window and got to dumping.

The car sped off as I began shooting back along with Scooter. I paused the video to see if I could get anything off the license plate and all I could see was one letter and three numbers. It wasn't much but it was clear enough for me to screenshot it. I wanted to send the image to Dudas but I was sure his hands were still full with what happened in the projects. Pulling up my dummy email account, I emailed Monk Man the image along with the level of urgency in the subject matter.

"Alright, I'm all done," Bri announced. "The bullet went through and through so I didn't have to do anything crazy." She stood and pulled off the latex gloves she'd put on.

"Thanks, Bri. You can go in my bathroom and clean your hands.

Oh, and there's a bottle of bleach under the sink. Fill the sink with a little water and bleach and put the tools you used inside." She nodded and went to complete the tasks.

Justice slowly sat up and I was able to get a good look at his bare chest. With the exception of the bandage that Bri skillfully attached to his skin, the tattoos that adorned his body made me want to clear the room and see about him. Sucking in a deep breath to regain my composure, his voice snapped me from my daze.

"I need to speak with you in private, beautiful," he said and I knew that wouldn't go over well with my people.

"Cute, but not an option," Tiff spoke for me.

He set his gaze on me and I shrugged my shoulders. Whatever he had to say to me, I'd be relaying to them at some point anyway, so there was no need to prolong it.

"Aight, cool. I need to know what type of shit you into before I insert myself in your business."

"And how you figure it's some shit she got going on?" Mo pressed. "You just popped up and some shit popped off. We were over here minding our business."

"And that may very well be the case, shorty." Wincing, he stood up as best he could and began to put his t-shirt back on. Unlike the coat and sweater, it didn't have blood on it. "Only I didn't just pop up, I was invited."

He had a point there, I said to myself.

"So, what you saying?" Tiff inquired, her eyes low in an attempt to figure out what angle he was coming from.

"I'm saying, I've been out of the game for four years and I ain't had no run ins since then. Not to say that a nigga's past can't or hasn't crept into the present, but I can't think of anyone that'll wanna take me out. Not without me getting them first. What about you, beautiful?"

"Shoot, your guess is as good of mine. Everyone loves me." I smirked and his lips stayed straight, not finding my humor humorous. "We'll get to the bottom of it and I'll be sure to keep you updated on where we are. I'm sorry that you got caught up in whatever this is." I was sincere in my apology.

"While I appreciate that, it won't be necessary. I got hit by a bullet by someone who seems to be gunning for you. If I wasn't interested in getting to know you before, I'm damn sure about to now." He picked up the remaining bloody clothing and walked to the door, making sure to pace himself.

"Hey, Justice," I called out and he turned slightly to look over his shoulder, "I can be a very dangerous woman."

He nodded his head. "Cool, cause I'm known to be a very dangerous man. Justice Blackstone, look me up if you must. Y'all have a safe night." He proceeded to leave the room, closing the door behind him.

I heard throat clearing, and Bri stepped out of the bathroom fanning herself. "Anyone else wet? Cause that smooth talking nigga there got me feeling some type of way."

My eyes stayed glued to the door. I would surely be looking into this Justice Blackstone. Something told me he was someone I wanted to know.

CHAPTER TWELVE – MORAE

We didn't expect the night to end peacefully after what had gone down, but we also didn't expect the club to be swarmed with so many police soon after Justice made his exit. The good ol' boys in blue interviewed the employees while we stood off to the side tightlipped. Mahogany had prepared her staff for different incidents that might occur and how to conduct themselves if cops came knocking. They knew what to say and what not to say. And they'd signed a contract stating just that when they got hired. We weren't worried about anyone talking.

Another 30 minutes passed before my brother, Dudas, pulled up on the scene in his signature black Dodge SRT Challenger. Money made sure he was gone before any police arrived. I sighed knowing that Dudas was going to have something unpleasant to say about all that had taken place. Although I knew I wouldn't be fond of his choice of words, I also knew that with him showing up it would clear the police presence instantly. I watched as he spoke to the cop who'd seemed to be the head person in charge that had arrived first. Whatever my brother had said, the cop nodded his head and gathered his officers to leave.

"Preciate you, Parks," Dudas spoke. "And if you could send over the statements you've collected thus far, I'd appreciate that too." The cop nodded and left the building with the rest of the little piggy's. Once the club was cleared of the pork smell, Dudas made his way over to us. He went to say something and Hogany held her hand up for him to stop.

"Gimmie a second," she said. "Scooter, let everyone know that we're closed for the night and I'll be sending out a text sometime in the morning." Scooter nodded and went to carry out her instructions. "Let's go to my office."

"Y'all kill me, wanting to talk privately after showing y'all ass publicly," Dudas let out with a shake of his head.

"So, you'd rather us talk out in the open, Detective?" I asked, smartly. Instead of responding, he fell in step with Mahogany with me and Tiffany bringing up the rear.

"Forreal, when y'all gon' stop this shit?" He started in on us before the office door was fully closed. The frown etched on his face displayed his disappointment. "While y'all out here having shootouts and shit, I'm down in the department trying to keep y'all names off the radar. The fuck happened here tonight?"

"I was wondering when you were going to get to that part. As usual, you're making assumptions versus asking questions and that ain't gon' help neither one of us." He hadn't been in my presence for five minutes and already he was pissing me off.

"Am I correct to assume there was a shootout that took place here?" He questioned with an accusatory look.

I closed the space between us, getting in his face. "A shootout would imply that we were in some kind of gun fight with a bunch of niggas in the street. Is that what you think occurred?"

"Ungh, ungh," Tiffany pulled me back, "we don't have time for that shit."

"Exactly," Mahogany chimed in. "The only thing we need to be focused on is the who. I don't even give a fuck about the why. Dudas, you not here for no reason so what you got for me?"

"Shit so far. I heard the call over the radio and came straight here. This shit is not good. This place was supposed to be peaceful territory, Mahogany. We all agreed to that."

"Nigga, you think I wanted someone to come here and shoot at me? I know what we agreed to."

"Exactly," I snapped.

"Aight. Well, I'ma look into it and see what I can find out. You think it may have something to do with what happened over there in those projects?" He was prying but Mahogany wouldn't take the bait.

"That's for me to know eventually and for you to find out now," she replied.

He shook his head and scoffed. "Yeah, sounds like something you'd say. I'ma hold up my part of the agreement as always, though. Whatever moves y'all plan on making next, please just keep the shit quiet, damn."

"I'll see to it that we do our best, Dudas. You have my word," Tiffany assured him. Her assurance may have worked too because according to him, amongst the three of us, she was the only person that took his concerns into consideration.

"Thanks, Tiff. Let me go and handle this shit. Can you walk me out to my car?" He asked me. I wanted to say no but Tiffany nudged me forward.

I walked out in front of him and in silence until we got outside. The parking lot was empty with the exception of his car, mine, Tiffany's, and Mahogany's.

"Wassup?"

"How you been?"

"Good. Working and living life. You?"

"I'm good but I'd be even better when you make the decision to walk away from this. You don't really have to do this shit, Mo. None of y'all have to do this shit forreal. It's so much shit y'all could be pouring y'all energy into that's productive. This right here ain't it."

I cocked my head to the side. "Has it ever occurred to you that we may just like what we do?"

"And why would you like having to live in a world where shit can come crashing down at any time, Morae. That shit don't make no sense."

"Same way you like living in a world where they kill men and boys that look like you every day. With all the judging you doing, you would think you had an occupation that can somehow save the world, Maurice."

"The difference between what I do and what you do is that I'm not aiding in the downfall of my community, Morae. Mommy didn't raise us to be on the type of shit you on."

"Nigga, mommy raised a hustla. What hustle I choose is my business. I'm your sister, you supposed to love me anyway. Just like I love you in spite of you working for them people. I can't keep having this kind of interaction with you every time we come into contact with each other, Dudas. This shit is draining." I sighed because no matter how many times we had this conversation, the outcome was still the same.

"You right, I'ma drop it. Hopefully, you'll actually listen and take heed to what I have to say. I would hate for it to be too late." He gave me a half hug and pecked my forehead. "Love you."

"Love you too, brother." I watched as he hopped in his car and drove away slowly. His words weren't cause for concern. He felt how he felt and vice versa. So long as he kept up his end of our agreement, I was straight.

Back in Mahogany's office, she had traded her club fit for jeans, a hoodie, and Gucci platform boots. Both her and Tiff were loading their guns and tucking them into their waists.

"Everything good with the two of you?" Tiffany asked while handing me a semi-automatic Glock-19.

Smiling hard, I examined the gun in all of its splendor as if I'd never seen it before. "Nothing's changed from any other interactions we've had. He expressed his feelings about what we do, I said how I felt, we said I love you's, end of story."

"How long you think he gon' be okay with being our inside man?" Tiffany followed up.

"Honestly, I know for a fact that the only reason why he still down is because he don't wanna see us take that trip Upstate. Other than that, he'd rather not be apart of it." I gave her the short version of my answer.

"So long as it stays that way, I ain't trippin'. And as much as I'd like to expound on the subject matter, we don't have the time,"

Hogany expressed. "Right now, we got a partial plate and no suspect list—."

"Okay, bitch, now you giving me Detective vibes," I cut her off. "Talkin' bout, suspect list. Please, okay."

"Watching too much damn, "Law & Order"," Tiffany added, agreeing with me.

"Shut up," Hogany said while laughing and lightening the mood a bit. "I sent what I could make out of the plate of the car to Monk Man. I'm not sure what he'll be able to do with it or if he'll be able to find anything. In the meantime, I want everybody at the spot in an hour. Whoever fails to show up will be number one on my hit list. I don't give a fuck what they got going on. If they're not on their death bed then I expect to see their face."

"On it." Pulling out my burner phone, I sent out a mass text to the lieutenants letting them know that we were holding an emergency meeting in an hour, no exceptions. Tucking my phone back in my pocket, I looked back and forth between Hogany and Tiffany.

"Just so y'all know, anybody say anything stupid or out of the way, I'm shooting first and asking questions later," Tiffany announced.

I nodded because I was on that same type of time. "Quick question, and this didn't cross my mind till now," I mentioned.

"Let's walk and talk," Hogany suggested. She shut down her office and we made our way out the door.

I picked up where I'd left off. "Ol' boy that came here looking for you, do you think he could've been behind this? I mean, the nigga popped up out of nowhere wanting to talk to you. Tiff blocked that... you think he felt away about it?"

"Enough to shoot at her?" Tiffany questioned, skeptical.

"Shit, we've shot at people for less. It's a respect thing, and you know how these men are with their egos."

Hogany stopped in front of her car and leaned against the passenger side door. "That did cross my mind. Everybody is a suspect though and guilty until proven innocent. Even those that just appear out of thin air, claiming to be kin to me."

My phone vibrated twice in my pocket and I went to check it. It was a text message from Monk Man. "Well, we'll have the answers in the morning. Monk Man just started the search."

"Cool, until then, let's get to this meeting. Always rule out things on the home front before seeking answers outside. Sometimes it's the ones closest to you." She hopped in her car and me and Tiffany walked over to ours to do the same.

She was right, it usually was the ones closest to you that you had to watch out for. I was happy to say that I didn't have to worry about my family going against me in any form or fashion. I wouldn't know how to respond if they did.

CHAPTER THIRTEEN — MAHOGANY

I leaned over the head of the conference table, using my long arms for leverage and looked each man that sat in their respective places in the eye. It was a little after two in the morning and while some faces showed they'd rather be elsewhere, others showed utter confusion. It was unlike me to call a meeting this late because I respected their time, but after what had gone down, I didn't give a fuck if I woke a nigga up out of a wet dream. I needed to get some shit figured out.

"Thanks for coming out fellas. I'm gonna get right to it because it's late and like myself, I know y'all have lives. Mine is very precious to me in fact. That said, a motherfucka tried to take it tonight." I paused to see everyone's reaction and found myself pleased.

Each slouched body sat up straight and all eyes were now alert. It was a good sign but I still needed to pick their brains.

"Wait, what? Fuck is you talkin' bout, Mahogany?" Briscoe's facial expression matched his tone... heated.

"Someone shot at me at my club earlier tonight. And while I wanna bet money it didn't come from anyone's camp in this room, I'd be crazy not to cross every T and dot every I. In my position, I think you all would understand that." By the murmurs in the room, I could tell that they were offended by my statement. I was gonna keep it a stack though.

"We ain't had nothing to do with that shit, Mahogany." Briscoe spoke on behalf of the collective. "We don't gain shit by you being dead, especially me."

"I ain't gon' bullshit you Mahogany, a nigga offended that you would even think that," Trick spoke up. "And then to call a meeting about it. Come on, we've been in business too long to crash out and do some dumb shit like that. And that goes for me and my people. I vouch for them all."

"Oh yeah," I commented, "even dude who Mo had to sit down?"

"Yeah," he responded, quickly, "even him."

My eyes scanned the room and each person nodded their heads in agreement with what Trick said except for Pete.

"So, wassup Pete?" Tiffany beat me to acknowledging his silence.

"Ain't shit. I'm just taking everything in," he said smoothly.

"Pete," I spoke, "if you recall, I made a stop in Harlem last week to handle some personal business. You would tell me if that business had any loose ends that needed to be addressed, wouldn't you?" Taking my gun from my hip, I put it on the table and turned the barrow so that it was facing him.

"Indeed. We've grown enough for you to know the type of nigga I am as well. Had I heard any noise, it would've been silenced before I brought it to your doorstep. You know how I am about family."

I nodded. "I know what you've shown me, I can't account for what's in your heart." Picking the gun up, I tucked it away. "Okay, I have the reassurance I need for now. Understand that my people are actively looking into this and sleep will not come easy for a lot of motherfuckas. With that said, if you hear so much as a whisper about what went down, I want it brought to me first."

Once I received head nods of understanding, I dismissed the meeting and everyone but Briscoe got up to leave. Mo and Tiffany escorted the guys out, giving me the opportunity to speak to him in private.

"What the fuck you got going on that you're getting shot at,

Mahogany? And why I gotta find out amongst the rest of these niggas?"

"It was no use in telling you beforehand when I had Mo send out a text for a meet up. You're a part of the coalition, aren't you?"

"I'm apart of this shit but outside of it, we have something that runs deeper than this Table. If something happens to you, I'm responsible for our daughter, Mahogany. Soon as that shit went down, I should've been notified."

"I hear you. I'll be sure to inform you first next time."

"Okay, you wanna play. This shit ain't no game! Did you see the nigga that bussed at you?"

I shook my head. "No, the shooter was hanging out the window of a car. I don't know whether it was a man or a woman. I'll find them though."

"Yeah, well, I'ma put my people on it too." He got up from his seat and got closer to me. "We may not always see eye to eye but I love you, Mahogany. You're Beautii's mother and your safety is everything to me."

"I appreciate that, Briscoe, but can you back up a little?" We took a step back at the same time. He was way too close and I could almost predict his next move. It wasn't that type of party.

"Are we interrupting?" Mo asked as she and Tiff returned.

"Nope," I spoke up. "Briscoe was just leaving."

"Yeah," he said, but his body hadn't moved.

"You're still standing there, Briscoe," she reminded him.

"I'll let you know what I find out. You keep me in the loop too." I didn't verbally agree to his request, I simply nodded.

With the way Briscoe had been acting, I wasn't convinced that he wasn't secretly preying on my downfall. And while I knew he wouldn't want me hurt or even worse, dead, I was sure he had no problem with seeing me shaken up. Too bad for him and anyone else that thought the same, Wright blood flowed freely through my veins. A real bitch wasn't shaken easy.

My phone rang next to me as I laid in bed, looking up at the ceiling. I'd only slept for two hours after arriving home a little after 4 a.m. I couldn't get the shooting out of my head. Like, someone really tried to take me out. And a normal person would probably be scared, but me, I was pissed the fuck off because why would someone even play with their lives like that? Deep in thought, I reached for my phone and it stopped ringing before I could answer it.

Checking to see who the missed call was from, I quickly dialed the number back. It was my father calling from one of his burner phones. Placing a few pillows behind my back, I sat up in bed. The phone rung four times before the call connected.

"Hey, dad."

"Tell me everything that happened from the beginning til' the time you got home." His tone was serious and I knew this wasn't his normal check in call.

I wasn't surprised that he'd reached out about it. I just wanted to be the one to tell him my account of what had gone down before he heard it elsewhere. The streets had a way of either reporting false info or factual info with their own twist. It was the last thing I wanted, especially when the events involved me getting shot at.

"In a nutshell—."

"No, Mahogany," he cut me off, "everything from the time you stepped outside til' the time you reached home at 4:17 this morning."

When he mentioned the time, I knew he'd spoken to my mother who hadn't gone home yet. Without further delay, I went over my night from the time me and the girls arrived at the club, to the conversation I had with Justice, and then the shooting. I'd told him about Justice during our last visit so he was familiar with the name.

"So, what do you know about the car?" He questioned.

"Nothing much, yet. I gave what I had from the plate to Monk Man to look into."

"The car is registered to Journey Williams. The address should be coming to your phone shortly. When shit like this happens, I don't expect to hear about it from a third party."

"I understand. How'd you get the information though?" It was a head scratching moment. While I knew my father had people who looked out for me, if someone was that close to see how everything played out, why not give me the information needed to start the process of my retribution? The phone went silent for a few seconds. "Dad?" I called out, making sure he was still on the line.

"You had a guest last night at the club, yes?"

My mind drew a blank for a second, then I remembered the guy Tiffany had talked to that asked to speak to me. "I did, but what does that—Dad, what's going on?"

"That was your brother, Santana. He's in town from Cali and I sent him your way on the business tip, he—."

"Wait, wait, hold on," I interjected. "My brother? Since when did I have a brother?" I didn't have the capacity for the Lifetime movie shit.

"He's your older brother, Mahogany. Mommy will have to explain it more. We already had a conversation. I gotta go, but look, don't allow the motherfucka who tried to take you away from me live another 24 hours. I don't give a fuck who you gotta touch to get to him or her, just get it done."

I stayed silent, biting the inside of my cheek in an attempt to calm my anger. He just dropped a bomb on me and left it in my mother's hands to deal with the aftermath. I had questions that needed answers.

"I'm on it, daddy. Love you."

"I love you more. And don't be so hard on your mother. We had our reasons."

"Lata, daddy." I ended the call before he could so that he knew I was in my feelings.

As I sat stewing, the text message came through with information for a 29-year-old, Journey Williams. I forwarded the message in my group chat with Tiffany and Mo and told them to meet me at the address in two hours. Two hours was enough time for me to get dressed and pick my mother's brain about her son. I couldn't claim him as family yet because I didn't know the nigga. And if I was being honest with myself, I wasn't sure if I wanted to know him.

"Good morning, mother." I entered the kitchen where my mother sat at the breakfast nook, nursing her morning cup of tea.

I'd taken a shower and got dressed after sitting in bed another 20 minutes processing the news my dad had laid on me. In the shower, the word brother kept playing in my head. How the hell had I been on this earth for 29 years and not know that I had a brother? That wasn't some shit that you just grow up not knowing without someone ensuring that you didn't know. Thinking on it so hard, my already sore head hurt more so I popped two Advils before approaching my mother.

"Don't come in here on that slick bullshit, Mahogany. If we gon' have a conversation, let's have a conversation. You have some hunting to do so I'll make it quick. We can really get into the details later." It was just like her to take control of the conversation before it could fully get started. I couldn't even be mad cause I was just like her.

"Well, since you already spoke to daddy, you already know what I wanna know." I pulled out one of the barstools and made myself comfortable. "Go head and tell the story, and you can add some details, I have a lil' bit of time."

She took a slow sip from her teacup and sat it back down. "Your brother's name is Santana Coast. He's seven years older than you. Daddy is not his biological father but has always treated him as such since we first got together when Santana was a year old. Santana's father got locked up shortly after I found out I was pregnant and went down for a ten-year bid. Like a real bitch, I held it down for the better part of a year and planned to ride the bid out until he started to make me feel like I was in the cell with him. I think the nigga was trying to stress me to the point where I'd lost my glow. I shut that shit down immediately. I still had a life to live and now a child to care for. So, I went on my way and still made sure his books were straight while no longer being emotionally available. I embraced my new role as a mom and met daddy." Her eyes twinkled mentioning my dad. It was cute. "We get together, he takes Santana in as his own, and we're a family. Now, even though daddy was now in my life, I made sure to keep Antwon up to date on his son's life. I sent pictures, and they talked on the phone. When he was released after 10 years, he made a life for himself out in California."

"Sorry to cut you off ma, but where do I fit in all of this? How is it that I don't remember seeing this Santana person around?"

"You were young, Hogany. You and your brother had a bond. He was very protective of you. Always wanting to hold you and feed you." She chuckled but I noted the sadness in her eyes. "I can show you some pictures that I have back at the house. Let me finish though. A year after Santana's father being home, he decided that he'd missed out on enough of Santana's life and wanted to step in as he stepped into his preteen era. Till this day, I regret my decision to allow my son to move to Cali. He became this Coast person that I didn't recognize. Daddy kept eyes on him while he was there and he was out in Long Beach wildin' and has been doing so since then."

"So, he didn't come back to visit? Why don't I remember him?"

"Shit, I tried to drag his lil' ass back here but he was getting up in age and daddy told me I had to let him make his own decisions as a young man. I did and he chose to stay there. We spoke on the phone often and eventually that communication dwindled. I cried many nights about it. Daddy hated that shit but he said when Santana was ready, he'd realize that he needed me just as much as he needed the streets." She reached out and grabbed my hand. "I could've done a better job at ensuring the bond between you and your brother remained untouched. I see now that I kept you away from him because I was hurting and I didn't want him to leave you feeling the way I feel now."

I covered her hand with mine and rubbed it. "That wasn't your decision to make, mommy." Getting up, I went to leave the kitchen.

"He reached out to me. We're gonna meet up at my house this evening for dinner. He has a daughter Beautii's age."

"Okay, I'll be back before then or I'll have Briscoe pick her up if I'm not."

"Really, Mahogany?"

"Respectfully, ma, that is your son. To me, he's just another nigga in the street. You made that decision for me, remember. Text me and let me know what time the dinner is." I left the kitchen and headed for the door.

She'd given me an earful. I basically had a sibling that was hidden from me for a reason that wasn't good enough for me. Not only did I have a problem in the street I had to address but now I felt like my family life was shaky. I couldn't have that. The Wright family would have a meeting as a whole sooner than later.

Arriving at the address of Journey Williams, I sent a text to the girls, letting them know that I was parked across the street from the apartment building. Mo texted back immediately that both her and Tiffany were parked on the corner in Monk Man's car. I waited until I saw them get out before doing the same. Noticing their all-back attire, I nodded in approval. They always thought ahead which I appreciated.

Although it was early in the morning, the sky had a dark hue to it, indicating rain soon. It worked to our advantage because there weren't any people hanging outside of the building. There were passerbys going about their day, likely not caring about the three black women dressed in all black, moving with purpose. No words were spoken as we met at the building and I rang buzzer four.

"Who?" A voice aggressively answered on the other hand. I couldn't make out whether it was a man or woman.

"Amazon. I have a package for a Journey Williams," I said the first thing that came to mind. There was silence and then the door buzzed, allowing us entry.

As much as people shopped online, Amazon could always get you in the door. The building looked decent inside, and I searched to see if there were any visible cameras around.

"Camera in the far-right corner, elevator over here," Tiffany pointed out. Precise as always.

She guided us to the elevator and I pressed for the fourth floor. The elevator was silent as Tiffany handed me and Mo a pair of black leather gloves. Something told me that we'd need it. I nodded, signaling my thanks just as the elevator dinged and opened on the fourth floor. I checked my phone again to ensure we were heading to the right door. Verifying we were going to apartment 4A, we turned a corner and were right in front of the door. I rang the bell and without confirming that I was in fact Amazon, the person on the other side opened the door enough to allow me to push my way inside.

"Bitch, what the fu—." The young woman yelled out.

My hand wrapped around her neck, making her words get caught in her throat. I hadn't identified the woman as Journey yet, but I didn't like the tone and I was very sensitive about that bitch word.

"Is your name Journey?" I asked, in a tone that didn't match my current action. It was rather pleasant. She grabbed at my hand and I loosened my grip enough for her to speak. "Girl, I have about as much patience as you have hair," I said, referencing the fro on her head that was in desperate need of combing. "Is your name Journey?" I heard a clicking sound behind me. By her widened eyes, I knew then that she knew it was serious. "That's the sounds of someone with no patience. Journey?"

She nodded, given me the confirmation I needed. I let her go and she fell to the ground, gasping for air. I let her for a few seconds till it became over the top.

"Bitch, we get it. Chill the fuck out," Mo said, annoyed.

"Journey, you own a black 2018 Acura, yes?"

"Uh, huh," she answered. The nervousness was evident in her voice but I wasn't here to ease her nerves. I was here for answers.

"We're off to a good start. Is this your license plate number?" I pulled up the picture of the full plate that I now had from Monk Man. Standing over her, I showed her the picture.

"Yes."

"Cool, someone in this car shot at me last night." I pulled my gun and we all surrounded her.

"Wait! Wait! I don't know anything about that. I let my boyfriend borrow my car last night, I swear." Tears immediately fell from her eyes as she scooted back on the floor with her hands up.

"What's his name?" I asked, screwing my silencer on.

"He didn't shoot at you. I don't even know you. Please, I swear to God I don't know what's going on."

"For someone who don't know what's going on, you sure crying hard, mami."

"You have a gun in my face and y'all bust in my apartment for Christ sakes."

"Aht, aht, we didn't bust in here. You opened the door without verifying who was on the other end. I'm not here to teach you that life lesson though. Back to ya man, what's his name and where is he?"

Before she could answer, I heard the door open and then a male's voice. "Bae, tell me why this nigga—oh shit." He went to turn and run out but Mo was quicker, sending a shot to his leg. "Ahhh, shit." It slowed him down but he still tried for the door.

"Nah, nigga, you got company," Mo said. "Move again, I dare you."

From where I stood, I was able to make out the guy's small stature. He was about a foot shorter than his girl and he didn't give me shooter vibe. Then again, a lot of cold-blooded killers didn't look like cold blooded killers.

"Who the fuck are y'all and what y'all doing in my crib? Goddamn, this bitch shot me."

I looked up at Mo and she aimed at his other leg. I shook my head and she lowered her piece at her side. "You lucky, nigga," she spat and kicked him in his leg, making him cry out again.

"We don't have all day for this shit," Tiffany finally spoke. She put her gun to Journey's head and the girl closed her eyes tightly and I could tell she was holding her breath. "Who was driving the black Acura and dumping shots at a club last night? Answer the mother-fucking question or Ima fill her body with lead."

"Jason," Journey slowly dragged out his name. "Tell these people whatever they wanna know."

"My leg man, just give me something to wrap my leg up and I'll tell y'all. I don't wanna bleed out." He rocked back and forth, holding his calf.

Phew! I sent a bullet to his left leg. "Just so you know how serious I am. The next one is going to be your head. Talk, nigga!"

He groaned and rolled over on the floor. "I let...my cousin borrow the car. He still has it now. Please, I need—." Phew, phew. I sent an additional two shots to his chest, killing him instantly.

Hearing Journey's stifled scream, I turned to face her. Her face was beet red and she was shaking. Bending down so that I was eye level with her, I snapped my fingers in her face. "Hey, look at me." Her eyes quickly snapped in my direction. The fear dripped from her body. If I wasn't already in savage mode, I would've probably felt bad for her. I had to think about my child though. The fact that she could've been motherless made me not give a fuck. "I'm sure you don't wanna see me again, so you know to keep this between us, right." She quickly nodded her head. "Great. Sorry you had to get caught up in this mess. Going forward, you must watch the company you keep. Borrowing your car just to let the next nigga drive it is crazy. Now, when the police get here, you let them know that two guys rushed in here and jumped on you and umm..."

"Jason," Tiffany helped me out.

"Yeah, you and Jason. Jason tried to fight one man off and shots ring out. Next thing you know, you were knocked unconscious."

"Huh?" She questioned through tears just as Tiffany hit her on the head with the butt of her gun.

"Let's go. Mo, call Monk Man and have him put in an anonymous call to 911 and report shots fired. Let Dudas know we have a body coming his way and to be on the scene. I need to track down that car."

"I got you," she confirmed as we walked towards the steps.

"Savage, huh?" Tiffany asked.

"These motherfuckas don't know who they playing with, Tiff. They sure gon' find out, though."

CHAPTER FOURTEEN – TIFFANY

"Did you get a chance to give Monk Man the name of car wash dude?" I asked Mo as we hopped in her car.

"Who, Justice?"

"Yeah."

"I did but I didn't feel like it was more pressing than this so I didn't tell him to expedite it." She pulled out of the parking spot and followed Mahogany's car as it passed us.

"Pressing, no, important, yes. I don't have the feeling that he was behind the failed hit but I would like to know who he is if he's gonna be around."

"How you figure he's gonna be around?"

"The last nigga she fucked with heavy and brought around us was Briscoe. She's been keeping phone time with this dude and I know you picked up on how they interact with each other."

"True, but—."

"Wait, ain't that the black Acura from the club that just passed us?" I cut her off and quickly dialed Mahogany's number.

"What, how you know?" Mo questioned, bussing a quick U-turn in the street as if it were legal to do so.

I didn't answer her but gestured with my hands for her to slow down and keep pace with the car. "I see the black Acura and it's headed in the direction we just came from. I bet he's dropping the car back off. Remember dead man said he let his cousin borrow the car and he hadn't got it back yet." I put the phone on speaker.

"Bitch, you lying, I'm turning right now. Are y'all behind him?"

"We are now."

"Good, crash into the car."

"Bitch, what?!" Mo exclaimed. "No, we not doing that. This my favorite car, and it's broad daylight. Come on now, be logical Mahogany."

"He's slowing down in front the building," I said. "Shit, you hear the sirens? Oh wait, he must've heard 'em too cause he ain't stop."

"Okay, let's just follow him closely. I got another call." She ended the call and we did as she said.

"You think whoever was behind the shooting knows what they've gotten themselves into?" Mo asked me.

"I'm almost positive they don't. And what's gonna piss her off even more is if she don't get to the source and it delays this expansion."

"Well, we're not gonna let that happen, Kelly."

"You damn right we're not, Michelle." I held my fist up and she smacked it down.

"Bitch, please, ain't no Michelle over here. This main character energy." I chuckled and she rolled her eyes. "Where is this nigga taking us?" She asked out loud, as the Acura swerved onto the highway without signaling. "Oohh, bitch, this nigga don't know how to drive. Lemme put my motherfuckin' seatbelt on."

"No, he knows how to drive. He also knows we're on to him so he's tryna shake us." I reached over to secure my seatbelt as well. I called Hogany back and the phone didn't fully ring before she answered.

"I was just about to call you."

"Yeah, he's on to us."

"Okay, I'm three cars behind y'all so just keep a safe distance. I don't give a fuck if we gotta follow this nigga to Canada. Something ain't sitting right with me and the answers are in that Acura. So, the sooner we get to him, the —." Skrrrr, BOOM!

"Oh, shit!" Me and Mo yelled out at the same time as we watched the Acura get hit by a loading truck and smacked into a guardrail.

"What the fuck?"

"We gon' be here for a while but the black Acura is done for," I let her know.

"Fuckkk!" She yelled out and the call went dead.

I glanced over at Mo who still had her hands gripped tightly around the steering wheel. The car behind us beeped us along and I had to tap Mo to get her attention. As we slowly drove past, I could see a part of the damage and it was bad. The car was smashed against the guardrail and I couldn't see the driver. Shaking my head, I texted Hogany that we were getting off at the next exit. It was safe to say that things had gone from complicated to fucked up. We'd just lost our lead.

Deciding we needed to regroup, we headed to Mo's place since we were closer to her. When we got there, Money was in her living room playing the game along with Monk Man and Paris' son.

"Hey, y'all," I spoke, entering the living room. "Look at you, handsome face."

"Thank you, baby," Money said, standing up to hug me.

"Now you know I'm not talking to you." I dodged his hug and picked DJ up from the couch. He hugged me tight around my neck and I tickled him, making him buss out in a fit of laughter.

I loved kids. DJ was the sweetest two-year-old you could ever meet. He was cool, like he'd been here before. I'd never heard Mo complain about him being whiney or even having that terrible two's stage parents talked about. He was just a joy to be around. Paris was doing a great job with him. As I went to put him back down on his feet, his shirt lifted up and I noticed a black and blue bruise on his rib. It wasn't huge but it was noticeable.

With a frown, I put his shirt down. He looked up at me and smiled before jumping back on the couch next to Monk Man. After giving Monk Man a hug, I finally turned to Money who had his arms out.

"You're a mess you know that." I walked into his embraced and he gave me a bear hug.

"Yeah, they say that."

"Where Paris at and why she leave my baby with y'all?" Mo asked.

"She upstairs taking a nap. She got here not too long before y'all, said she had a headache," Money answered.

"Mo!" DJ yelled out and ran off the couch at lightning speed towards Mo. She swooped him up in her arms and kissed his cheeks. I loved their bond.

"Wassup, Monk Man?" She spoke to her brother and he gave her a head nod. "Still on bullshit, huh? I love you, too. I'm gonna go check on Paris, get her a shot or something." She pointed behind her where Mahogany brought up the rear.

Her face was buried in her phone and she walked straight to the kitchen not saying anything to anyone. Money gestured to her and mouthed, "what happened?" I put my hand up to my mouth signaling for him to be quiet. I followed Mahogany to the kitchen and stopped when I heard her on the phone.

"Ma, I'm not comfortable with my daughter being around some-body I don't know. What I'm not understanding is why that's an issue for you. I don't know that man.... Okay, how bout this? I'll have Briscoe come get her early and then I'll meet at your house later." She ended the call and turned to me.

"Wassup?"

"Shit, drama. Nothing I can't handle though. I gotta figure out who's behind this shooting, Tiff. I mean, really, who could be gunning for me?"

"You mean we gotta figure that out, and we will. Ain't no doubt in my mind about that. In the meantime, let's not sit on our hands and move as normal. Something in me tells me that the person is gonna reveal themselves and it's closer than we think. What about this Santana person?" She gave me a blank look and walked over to Mo's wine collection she had set up in her kitchen. "Ahh hell, what bitch? And don't pour me nothing. You know I don't think straight when I'm pissed off and I got a feeling I may be just that or shocked."

"I ain't pouring you up, I'm doing this shit for me. I know I need it." She poured herself a glass of red wine and took a few sips. Taking a slow, deep breath, she hit me with some news. "Girl, that Santana nigga is my brother."

"You bullshittin'."

"No bullshit. I just found out this morning."

"Girl, ain't no way. I've known you all my life and ain't known you to have no siblings."

"It's clear that I didn't know, either. Ma said he moved out to Cali when I was younger. It still don't make no sense to me though because why don't I remember him?"

"Did he visit often?" I was scratching my own head tryna figure this shit out.

"I don't think so because we both would've seen him. Me and you have always been two peas in a pod."

"True. Damn, you got a brother." Even saying it aloud was unbelievable.

"Get this, it was my dad who sent him to the club to see me. And I think he was around to see the shooting."

"Why you say that?" Her assumption piqued my interest, and not in a good way.

"Cause when my dad called this morning, he already knew. Now, it's highly likely that he heard it through the grapevine but it's also a coincidence that my "brother" was at the club that night."

"Shit, you think he had something to do with it?" Now that she identified him as her brother, I erased the thought.

"No, but if he was around during the chaos, I'm wondering did the nigga at least buss back to help a bitch out? I did hear different guns."

I nodded my head in deep thought at the possibility. "It's possible."

"I'll find out tonight. He's gonna be at mommy's tonight for dinner with his girl and their daughter."

"Oh, that's what you were talkin' about on the phone."

"Yeah."

"I can watch my Beautii girl for you if you want. She can even spend the night. We can make it a girl's night, and she can do my make up since you was slick hating the last time."

"Really? That would work. I'll text mommy now and let her know."

"Cool. And hear me when I say we gon' find the person behind the shooting. Niggas ain't been playing with us like that, we ain't gon' let them think they can start now." She raised her glass and tilted it towards me.

"Glad you know." I left the kitchen and ran into Money. "Boy, you too grown to be ear hustling." I playfully pushed him back from me and he grabbed my arm, pulling me into the bathroom in the hallway. "Montez, what the hell—." He cut me off by smashing his lips into mine. Caught off guard, I froze until he used his tongue to spread my lips.

"I want you so fucking bad, Tiff. Open up and let a nigga in here." He whispered into my lips and I felt like putty in his hands. Sex should've been the last thing on either of our minds but here we were about to do this quickie in Mo's bathroom. I only hoped that she would forgive me after.

"Move back," I whispered to him. He gave me space enough to pull my shirt off and step out of my jeans.

Seeing how I was moving, he followed, only he didn't fully strip. When he pulled his shirt off, my clit thumped but when he pulled that dick out of his boxers, I creamed. It was a pretty cinnamon brown color with the prettiest mushroom head I'd ever seen. When I seen that his dick had a curve to it, I silently thanked God for the lashing I was sure he was about to put on my G-spot. I went to turn around and bend over only to be stopped by his hand on my stomach.

"Ungh, ungh, I want you to look at me while you take this big, black, motherfucka." He pushed me back slightly so that my ass was on the sink.

I jumped a little from the coolness but my body heated back up when I felt two of his fingers slide up and down my slit. My pussy leaked sweet cream with anticipation. The fact that my body was reacting to him in such a way was crazy. The euphoric feeling made me drop my head back, exposing my neck. Money took full advantage of the moment, placing his juicy lips on my neck, planting slow kisses before using his tongue to trace my jawline. This wasn't giving quickie vibes. This nigga was tryna make love to me in the bathroom.

"Put it inn," I cried out lowly. My eyelids felt heavy and I felt the urge to touch myself so I did just that. I pinched my nipples and stuck my tongue out for him which he happily accepted. Wrapping his hand around my neck, he slid into me slowly, filling me up inch by inch.

"Oooh shit, you betta gimmie dat dick, nigga... shit, yes." My shit talking encouraged his slow but methodically strokes.

It felt like he was hitting the bottom of my pussy the way he twisted his hips, making that curve tap at my G-spot. I lifted my leg onto the wall to give him more access. He took it into his arm and pounded me with precision.

"Fuckkkk, I knew she'd be wet like this for me. Damn, mama, work that shit." His teeth sunk into my neck and I fought the urge to scream out in ecstasy.

Instead, I bit my bottom lip and allowed him to take my body into his. I thrusted my hips upward, matching his movements and squeezing my walls, inviting him further in. My wetness seeped out of me down the crack of my ass and I could hear the sounds of my kitty kat. She was so wet; I was afraid to look down at the floor because we were definitely making a mess. Feeling an orgasm building up from my feet, I put my hand on my clit to play with it.

"Daddy got you, baby. You gon' cum for me?"

"Mmmm, yess, it's right there, Montez."

"Well, come on then. Rain down on your dick." He swiped his hand over my clit a few times, making it swell up, and I had to bite into his shoulder to muffle my scream of passion. "Uh huh, gimmie dat shit, girl." My body shook as I wrapped my arms around his neck and rained down on him. He continued to thrust in and out of me until he was right behind me. The shit was so powerful, it was as if I felt his nut as it left his body and lodged into my uterus.

We didn't get to bask in the moment for too long because there was a knock at the door that made my eyes widen.

"I hope y'all know Mo gon' kick y'all ass for fucking in her bathroom." Mahogany could be heard giggling on the other side of the door and I wanted to curse her out. I chose not to though, hoping that by us staying quiet, it'd be like what happened had never happened.

"You can unfreeze, bae, I think she walked off," Money said.

"Shut up." I hit him, he reached in to kiss me, and I let him. "Come on, we gotta get dressed." He slowly pulled himself out of me and he was covered in my essence.

"You wanna lick it off?" He asked, making his dick jump.

"I would, but we need to hurry up. Mo already gon' cuss us out."

"Man, we grown. Plus, she wants us to be together." I ignored him and proceeded to redress myself. Neither one of us bothered to wipe up. "You good?" He asked once we were both dressed.

"Yeah. And just because we fucked don't mean we together, Montez. We already talked about this," I let him know.

"You right, us fucking don't mean we together. Me just putting a baby in you does." He kissed my nose and walked out, leaving the door halfway closed.

This nigga was losing his mind. I wasn't pregnant because I couldn't get pregnant, he knew that. And although my lips were saying we weren't together, my heart was feeling something else. Unfortunately, I didn't have time for love. We had an expansion on the rise and an unknown shooter running around thinking he or she had one upped us. Yeah, the love shit would have to wait.

CHAPTER FIFTEEN – MORAE

When I walked into my bedroom, Paris was in the bed sleeping like Montez said she was. I did my best to creep through quietly with DJ on my hip but Paris was a light sleeper and could hear a rat piss on cotton.

"Mmm, what y'all doing creepin' through here?" She questioned with sleep in her voice.

"Hey, baby. I just came to check up on you. I'ma take him back downstairs, though."

"Wait, no kiss?"

"My bad," I said, walking over to the bed and leaning down to kiss her lips. My one tap wasn't good enough for her, though. She gave me four additional pecks and a kiss on my neck.

"Put down." DJ requested for me to let him go by trying to slide down my body. Laughing, I allowed him to. Before he got to the floor, a mark caught my eye.

"Wait, DJ, come here, papa." I caught hold of his arm before he could run towards our bedroom door. "Hey, have you seen this?" I asked Paris while lifting up his shirt. The room had a little light from the curtains being slightly opened, but I flicked on the room light so I could make sure my eyes weren't deceiving me.

I picked DJ up and sat him on my lap to get a better look. Seeing the slight black and blue bruise on his side, I bit the inside of my mouth to control my anger. I waited for Paris to talk but she was silent. Turning towards her, she didn't look me in the eye, only stared at DJ with a sad look on her face.

"How long has he had this bruise?" I asked her.

"For about a week."

I wanted to flip on her but I knew if I did, she wouldn't tell me what happened to him to cause the bruise in the first place. And that was something I needed to know. Taking a deep breath to calm myself, I sat an oblivious DJ down on the bed.

"Is that why he's been at your mom's house for the last couple days?" She nodded her head. "So, you lied when you said your mom wanted to keep him for a couple days?"

"No. That wasn't a lie. She did call me to get him. It just happened to be around the time that this happened."

"Aight, cool." I leaned over to kiss DJ on the forehead and rubbed his side before getting up and walking towards the door.

"Wait, Morae, we're not gonna talk about it?"

"If you wanted to talk about it, you would've told me when it first happened. Clearly you decided that it wasn't something I needed to know."

"Babe, wait, you know that's not fair. I didn't tell you because I didn't know how you would react and I took care of it. The last time y'all interacted with each other didn't go so well, and... baby, if I can avoid putting you in the mix of my shit, I will."

"Cool, I'll be back." I was heated and I knew if I stood in front of her too much longer, I'd end up blackin' on her. She climbed out of bed and started towards me but the look I gave her made her stop.

"I took care of it," she repeated.

"I heard you the first time. I'll be back." Leaving the room, I took the steps two at a time and when I reached the bottom, Mahogany and Tiffany were in the livingroom with Money and Monk Man. Disregarding their presence, I kept it moving.

"Mo, where you headed to?" Mahogany asked.

"I gotta run an errand," I answered without looking in her direction. "I'll be right back." Leaving my place, I hopped in my car and put DJ's grandmother's address in my GPS. Soon after I put my car in drive, the phone rang with an incoming call from Paris. Ignoring it, I silenced any incoming notifications from her.

I wasn't mad at her for what happened to DJ because I knew that she'd addressed it. I was more mad that she didn't feel the need to tell me. At the end of the day, we were in a relationship. I wanted to know everything she had going on, especially when it came down to her bd. At this point, he was taking for granted that I was a woman and had taken a backseat when it came to how they co-parented. We had the meet up when I came back from Colombia like I said we would, only it was over the phone.

I didn't feel like we got anything out of it because rather than get an understanding and come to a resolution about the pick-up and drop off, homeboy wanted to hang his nuts. He tried everything in his power to piss me off by saying slick shit but I stuck to the topic at hand, DJ. The conversation only really went left when he started to get disrespectful. At that point in time, I let it be known that I said all that I was gonna say and ended the call. I wasn't about to sit on the phone and argue with a grown ass man that didn't know how to communicate. If push came to shove, I'd murk his ass and that would be that.

Now, here we were. I was being put in a position where I had to defend what was mine. Was that a problem for me? No. It was gonna be a problem for his mother, though. I knew I couldn't beat no man, so I was gonna beat up the woman he loved.

My phone rang again, this time it was my brother calling. I wanted to ignore the call but remembered that business still had to be handled, and if he was calling he had to have an update on the shooting or shooter. I answered the call on speakerphone.

"Wassup, Dudas?"

"Yo, where's Monk Man?" He asked, with a sense of urgency in his tone.

"At the house, why?"

"Who's at the house with him?"

"Paris, Money, Hogany, and Tiff. Why?"

"There's a fucking warrant out for his arrest, Morae."

"A warrant out for his arrest?!" I exclaimed. "What the hell are you talking about?"

"According to the system, it's an abuse on a minor. The minor is Paris' son, Mo. His father is claiming that Monk Man has been abusing him."

"That motherfucka did wh—." My other line beeped with an incoming call from Money. "Dudas, hold on, this Money on the other line."

"Nah, Mo, we gotta address this shit."

"I know that, Dudas. Just hold the line, damn!" I clicked over before he could protest.

"Money, I got—."

"Get back to the house now! The motherfuckin' cops just came up in here and locked Monk Man up on some bullshit ass child abuse charges. Get here, Mo!" He hung up the phone and I saw red.

Changing my car's direction, I picked up speed to get back home. In my haste, I disconnected the call with Dudas. Quickly dialing back, he answered on the first ring.

"They just picked him up. Find out what precinct he's in and send me the information."

"No, we agreed that so long as y'all are into y'all shit, y'all are to have no contact with the police under any circumstances. I'll look into what's going on with Monroe."

Biting my lip hard enough to draw blood, I spoke through gritted teeth. "I don't give a fuck about no goddamn agreement. Find out where the fuck our baby brother is and send me the fucking information. He is not to spend an hour in jail. You see to it that he don't."

"I'm gonna get him out, Morae."

"Send the information, Dudas. And I'll handle the rest."

"What you mean, you'll handle the rest? The courts will deal with this. We know our brother would never hurt a kid."

"Dudas, you worry bout what you worry about and I'ma worry

about what I worry about, okay. One hour." Ending the call, I hit the steering wheel hard. I didn't know what the fuck was in the air but it smelled like fuckery. Clearly, it was time for me to get on some fuck shit.

CHAPTER SIXTEEN – COAST

"Ooh, shit, I'm about to cum. Ughh!" Renee was on top of me with beads of sweat rolling down her neck as she got her shit off for the second time since we'd been fucking the last 15 mins.

I was tryna put a hurting on that sweet ass pussy. Although it has been a little over a week since I'd been home and tore her shit up, I wanted to make sure everytime I was in it, she remembered why she waited.

"Let that shit go. Daddy gon' come right with you." I smacked her ass hard and the sound echoed throughout the hotel room we'd been occupying for the last couple days.

I'd brought Renee and our daughter Asia out to New York on the pretense that I was meeting up with my mother for a long overdue reunion. It was partly true but I also had to lay the groundwork on solidifying my rightful spot at The Table. Shit, if you ask me, the position as HNIC should've been mine the moment Coolie knew he was going up the road. I checked all the boxes. I wasn't green to the game, this shit was in me. I knew how to move, and above all, I was a man. That should've been the greenlight off top.

The fact that he had my sister out here holding court was crazy.

Call me chauvinistic but that wasn't a woman's place. Not saying she couldn't be a part of the game but on the front line, that was a no no. I figured that she and I could chop it up on some brother-sister type shit and she'd just take a step back and let a nigga takeover, but after putting a few ears to the streets through my connections, I found out that my lil' sister wasn't a lil' girl no more. She had a clique of thoroughbreds with her and their names rang bells. They proved that when her representative back at the club wouldn't allow me access to her.

I couldn't lie and say I didn't feel proud when I heard about how my sister carried herself. I ain't hear nothing about her being in the mix on no thot shit. Her name wasn't synonymous with being on no grimy shit, and what I appreciated most was the respect her name held. She had the qualities of a great leader but I just knew I'd be able to lead better, and I needed her to see it my way.

"Mmmm, sssss." Renee's moaning and hissing made me slow down my strokes and switch positions. Still inside her, I rolled her on her side, lifted her leg, and twisted my hips so that I hit each wall with precision. "Ohhh, God!" She cried out and after that last stroke and twist, we both reached our peak.

"I love you, girl."

"Mmm, I love you more, baby." Reaching up to touch my face, she kissed my lips twice and laid her head in the crook of my neck.

Before we could get comfortable, my phone rang. Reaching up to check it, I saw Razor's number. "Hold on a minute, bae, I gotta get this." She moved to the side, allowing me room to sit up. "Wassup wit it?" I answered once the call connected.

"Nigga, you ain't gon' believe this shit. Where you at right now?"

"The hotel with my family. Wassup, talk to me."

"Bro, I just pulled up to my son's building and this shit is a crime scene."

"Yeah, that nigga live in the Bronx, why you actin' like that's something new?"

He sucked his teeth. "Nah, nigga. I saw them bring his girl out on a stretcher and then someone out in a white sheet right behind her. I ain't gotta put no money up for someone to tell me that was him under that sheet."

"Say word?!" My voice went up an octave as I stood up from the bed.

"Word. Somebody got to 'em."

"Damn, have you tried to call his people?"

"You mean dude that was wit 'em last night?"

"Yeah."

"Yeah, I did but he ain't pick up. You think... nah nevermind. I know they ain't moving like that. Cause who would've—."

"Aye, lemme hit you back," I cut him off. The conversation was headed in another direction and I didn't want him saying anything crazy.

"Aight. I'ma keep trying to call his people and see what all we can find out. Might even go see about his girl too."

"Sounds like a plan, just keep me posted." We hung up and I sighed.

"Everything okay?" Renee asked. I turned to her and she was now sitting up with the sheet covering her body.

"Yeah, everything is straight. Might need to run out real quick and meet up with Razor though."

"Okay, remember we said we'd take Asia shopping today."

"Does Asia wanna go shopping or you wanna go shopping, love?"

"Both of us. I wanna get us both an outfit for when we go see your mother later. We're still going right?"

"Yep, so long as she doesn't cancel."

"She won't, baby. Come here." She beckoned me with her finger and I sat down on the edge of the bed. She put her hands on my shoulders and started to knead my back. "You think your sister will be there?"

"I'm hoping so. We have some catching up to do."

"You think she'll be open to the idea of letting you be in position and her being alongside you?"

I thought for a second before responding. "I'm sure she'll see it my way once I lay out the blueprint."

"I know how much it means to you, so I hope you're right." She kissed my ear. Grabbing her hand, I kissed the inside of it and pulled her around me so that she was sitting in my lap.

"The way I see it, it'd be better for her to have me as a brother than as an enemy." That little shit that happened at the club was just to see how she handled herself.

Judging by the way she snapped into action along with her people, I knew she was about her shit. Now I knew the angle I would work to get in her good graces while playing the role of the brother who wanted to be of assistance and help her continuing to build onto the Wright empire. She'd never see it coming once I swept her seat right from up under her.

We got to my mother's house five minutes ahead of schedule and sat outside of her gate in our car looking up at her estate. This was definitely two steps up from the house we lived in before I moved to Cali. And I thought our house we had then was something. This shit we'd pulled up to was exclusive.

"Wow, dad. Is your mother rich?"

"To tell you the truth, princess, I don't even know. I haven't seen my mom in years. I do know that while growing up, I wanted for nothing and got everything a kid could've ever wanted or needed and then some."

"Sounds like how you and mommy treat me." I looked up in the rearview mirror and winked at her. Asia was my twin. It was a fact that Renee only carried her because she had all of my facial features. She was every bit of a female Santana. My daughter was my heart and I was gonna see to it that she had the best childhood.

"That's right and it'll only get better."

"4 sho." Her reply made Renee giggle.

"That is your child forreal. You ready for this?" My hesitance must've been written all over my face for her to ask me that.

"As ready as I'll ever be." Picking up my phone, I dialed my mother's number and she answered on the second ring.

"I was beginning to wonder if you were gonna turn around and leave. You've been sitting out there for a few minutes."

"I ain't gon' lie, I thought about it. Then I figured after all this time, I needed to see this through." Renee eyed me, confused by my admission that I hadn't shared with her. I shrugged my shoulders and focused back on the phone.

"I see. Well, should I wrap this food up and take it over to a shelter or what, son?"

"What you cook?" I asked, further prolonging the face to face.

"Boy, if you don't get off my phone and getcho ass in this house!" She ended the call and the gates opened, allowing us to drive up her winding driveway.

As we got closer to the house, I eyed the cars parked in front of her garage. One that stuck out was the old school Corvette. I recognized the car that me and Coolie had worked on every Sunday morning before taking my mother out to breakfast. It was one of the ways we bonded. One of the memories I had stored in my memory bank when I thought about my childhood. Parking behind the car, I helped my girls out.

Walking up the steps, the door opened and my mother stood on the other side of it. Once we reached the top step, the entryway lit up. I half expected her to come to the door in some over the top ass evening gown acting all uppity and shit. The mother I knew was nothing like that but it had been some years and people change, I know I have. She came the exact opposite, though. Dressed in a pair of jeans, a silk button up shirt, and a silk head scarf. On her feet were a pair of designer heels. Some things haven't changed, I thought to myself.

"Wassup, ma?" I spoke casually.

She threw her hand on her hip and cocked her head to the side. "I know that's not the way you greet the mother you haven't seen in years. What y'all got going on out there in Cali? Better yet, what kinda bitches they got raising kids over there? No offense, love," she gestured towards Renee.

"Hey, none taken," Renee replied with her hand up. She nudged me and I walked up to the door to embrace my mother for the first time in years.

"Oh, cause you know I ain't gon' beg you to hug me. Especially not after I pushed you out of my ass."

"Mann, chill," I laughed. She squeezed me tight and rubbed my back in a circular motion. "I love you, ma."

"I love you too, son. Now, get back before you mess up my make-up." Stepping back, I watched her dab at her eyes. "And look at this pretty girl," she said to Asia.

"Hey, grandma," Asia greeted and walked into a hug. She too offered a tight hug that made my mother tear up.

"Oh, y'all wrong for this. Come on in the house so we can eat. Renee, right?"

"Yes," Renee responded. "It's nice to finally meet you."

"You too, sweetie." She gave her a peck on the cheek and stepped aside for us to enter. "The dining room is two rooms down on your left. The chef is putting out a few appetizers, get whatever you want. Hold on a second, Santana," she called out to me as I went to follow the girls.

"Go head, bae, I'm coming." I waved Renee forward.

I heard a car entering the driveway and turned to see who else she invited. The all-white Tesla slowly drove up and passed the garage to park directly in front of the driveway. My mother grabbed hold of my arm and off sheer instinct, I pulled away. The driver of the Tesla kept the car running for a few seconds before turning it off and exiting the car. I knew it was a female from the long hair and when she turned around, I immediately recognized my little sister's face. Only she wasn't the four-year-old I'd left all those years ago. This was my sister, the boss, head of The Table. And by the look on her face as she ascended the steps, dinner was sure to be interesting.

CHAPTER SEVENTEEN – MAHOGANY

"Wassup, beautiful?" Justice spoke into my phone as I left Mo's place.

"Hey, if you're calling for updates, let me stop you now." I was in no mood to be questioned about what I found out about the shooting. The day had already taken me for a loop.

"Chill, beautiful, I was actually calling to see how you were feeling. I'm bound to find out what I wanna know about last night once I'm ready."

"You're calling to see how I'm feeling? Aren't you the one that got shot?" Getting in my car, I put the phone on speaker and sat it in my center console.

"You're right, you should've been calling me but I ain't trippin'. Back to you, how are you feeling?"

I don't know why I had the urge to tell this man about my day, including finding out that I had a sibling. For some reason, I just wanted to put it all out there in an effort to clear my mind. No sooner than the thought left my mind, I quickly shook it. I had to remind myself of my position and even more I didn't know Justice like that. So, I said what came naturally.

"I'm good. Headed to tend to some family business at the moment. How are you?"

"Shit, alive. All praises to Allah."

"All praises to who?" I asked with my lip curled and a roll of my eyes. I hated when niggas played Muslim because it sounded cool.

"Allah."

"You Muslim?"

"I am."

"Mmmhmm."

He chuckled. "What's the mmhmm for?" The way he mocked me was so cute, I had to chuckle myself.

"I'm just saying, are you really Muslim?"

"I am."

"You know that pasta carbonara we had at that Italian restaurant had bacon in it, right?" I wanted to see if he knew I'd caught on to his bullshit.

"Nah, beautiful, yours had bacon on it. I requested mine without the swine. You would've seen that but you were too busy facing yours."

I laughed because now he was tryna play me. "No, I was not. Alright, I could've slowed down a bit, that shit was good, though." He laughed along with me and it felt good after the day I had.

"You have a beautiful laugh."

"Yep, and a killer smile, pun intended."

"Heard you, killer. Speaking of, have you figured out the plan for us to find out who shot me tryna get to you?"

"Justice, ain't no us in the figuring out. It's just me and my people."

"Well, tell me how is that fair when I'm the one gonna be walking around with scarring to reference said shooting?"

"Hey, ain't nothing a little cocoa butter can't fix."

"Damn, you insensitive."

"I..."

"Nah," he laughed, "I'm just fuckin' witchu. Forreal though, I only wanna be involved because I wanna be sure no shit like that ever happens again."

There were those butterflies. "It won't. You can bet ya last dollar that shit ain't gon' happen again," I declared.

"And I will, cause you've gained yourself a new friend that ain't gon' play about you."

"Is that right?"

"Damn straight."

"So, the shooting didn't turn you off from me? Back at the club you mentioned having been out of the game for a while."

"I have but it's still in my blood, you know what I'm saying."

"Actually, I don't. I'm an upstanding businesswoman." I smiled at myself in the mirror as the words left my lips.

"And who am I to refute that?"

"Right. But, hey, I've arrived at my destination. Can I give you a call later?"

"Yeah, that's cool. Aye, businesswoman?" He called out before I could end the call.

"Yes?" I responded with a giggle.

"Stay out of trouble, aight."

I paused before answering. "Sir, I am trouble. Have a goodnight." I ended the call just as I pulled up to my mother's house. Typing in the code to the gate, it opened and I drove up slowly. Getting closer, I noticed that she was standing in the doorway with the guy I'd seen last night at the club. I recognized him from the braids.

Taking a moment to pray for a decent outcome for this little pow wow, I turned my car off and got out. I prayed for the best but was prepared for the worst. Here goes fucking nothing.

"Hey, ma," I spoke to my mother, kissing her cheek once I reached the door.

"Hey, boo. This is Santana...your brother."

"Hey," I spoke dryly.

"Damn, look at you sis. When I last saw you, you were chasing me around the house." He smiled big and unfortunately, I was unable to share in the memory.

"Can't say that I remember that. We gon' stand at the door or we going inside?" My mother stepped back and gestured for me to enter. "Where's Beautii?"

"Upstairs in her room," my mother answered. After the unforeseen events that went down with Monk Man being picked up by the boys, the plan for Tiff to pick her up was cancelled.

"Who's Beautii?"

"Your niece," my mother spoke first.

"My daughter." She gave me a disapproving look and I matched hers. She just over here making people kin to my child, losing me.

"Oh, word? I have a nine-year-old princess myself. She's in there with her mother."

"Ma, can you get Beautii for me?"

"What? I thought you were gonna stay for dinner. I had Gennie cook up a whole bunch of food." She was disappointed but I wasn't in the mood to get along tonight. I thought I would be able to do it but my head was all over the place and in order to fully be able to be a part of the welcoming committee, my mind had to be right.

"Yeah, but I had a long day and I just wanna head home."

She sighed. "Alright, let me go get her."

"Ay, can I talk to you for a minute?" Santana asked once my mother was out of earshot.

"Is it regarding your visit to my club?"

"Yeah, does mama know?"

"Know what?" I inquired.

He looked over at the steps she'd walked up and back at me. "About you being in a shootout."

"She knows a lot. How much do you know?"

"Shit, I know somebody was on yo ass that night. Soon as I heard shots, I just started thumping. I ain't know where them shits was coming from until I seen yo' people bussin' at the car that sped off. I didn't know how you would feel about me being in yo shit when you hadn't verified who I was yet, so I peeled off instead of coming to check up on you. That would've been awkward as hell for me to just walk up asking if you were good, ya know."

"Yeah, I can see that," I responded skeptically.

"Yeah, so I just got in touch with Coolie so he could put you on game."

"Cool." If he was looking for a thank you, he was seeking that from the wrong person.

"Look, I know you really don't know me although I am your blood brother, but I'd like the opportunity to chop it up with you. Not just on the business tip but just to reconnect and shit. Shit, I'm doing the same thing with mama. I ain't seen her in years."

"The both of y'all made those choices. Don't put your guilt on me and use that as a reason to reconnect." My guard was up because again, I didn't know him and the circumstances surrounding him popping up was still strange to me.

"I get that. I'm just trying to make it right and after what went down last night, I feel like you could use your big brother for protection."

"Hey, mommy." Beautii walked downstairs with my mother closely behind her.

"Hey, twin." I hugged her and kissed her forehead once she made it over to me.

"I'll see you tomorrow, Babygirl," my mother said to Beautii and they hugged each other.

"Alright, Gran. I love you."

"I love you too, girlie. And I love you, Hogany. Call me when y'all make it home."

"Will do." She walked off, leaving me, Beautii, and Santana in the foyer.

"Who's this, ma?" Beautii inquired, staring at Santana as if she were sizing him up.

"I'm your—." He went to answer and I stopped him.

"That's grandma's son."

"Oh, your brother."

"No, grandma's son. Go out to the car, I'll be right behind you."

"Two things," I went to speak once Beautii was out the door. "I don't know you and you don't know me. We are complete strangers, who just happen to share a parent. You wanna build a relationship with me, we do it on my terms. Sounds like you may wanna do some business, there may be a spot for you but you'll go through a preliminary screening just like everybody else. Lastly, my protection comes in three's, two of which I keep on my person at all times, the third ain't never too far away."

"That sounds like the tone of a boss."

"The Wright one. Enjoy your night, Santana Coast." I walked out of the house, closing the door behind me. I don't know what plans were going through Santana's mind when he decided to come back to the East Coast, but he was on my turf and over here, we played by my rules. He'd soon see just what I meant by me being the Wright one.

TO BE CONTINUED...

Charge It To The Game 2
Coming Soon

KEEP READING FOR A PREVIEW OF...

A Setup For Revenge
By Ashley Williams

CHAPTER ONE – BABYGIRL

My name was Cameron, but everyone called me Babygirl. From my mother's womb until I was about eight years old, I'd always lived in small places. Due to my father's lifestyle, I'd been in and out of hotels all throughout the states. My father, Jonathan, was a pimp and a drug dealer. Before she was murdered, my mother, Wanda, was an addict but wanted to beat the addiction to crack so bad. At least she acted like it.

Along with being an addict, my mother was very evil. She let my father beat me and even tried selling me to his clients without a care in the world. I can't count how many times I'd ran away, wondering why my mother would do this to me. A mother was supposed to love and nurture her child, and with me being a young girl, one would think that would be my mother's sole purpose. Unfortunately, it wasn't.

Things only went from bad to worse as the years went by and as I grew older. Life became harder, and eventually, tragedy struck. My mother was unintentionally killed by my father. He had shot at an intruder who made his way inside our small home, and my mother was caught in the crossfire as she moved about our dark house to safety. She was shot in her chest and died instantly.

My father was arrested that night but was subsequently acquitted of murder charges after all twelve jurors found him not guilty. If you ask me, he should have gone to jail. The murder may have been an accident, but had my father not been involved with shady people who later became enemies, then maybe my mother would still be alive today. She may have done some dirty things and hurt me in ways no child should ever have to endure, but I still loved her. I thought about her often and found myself envisioning what life would have been like had she loved me just a little bit more.

Alice, one of my father's prostitutes, had been a part of my life for quite some time now and I just loved her. My father had been cheating on my mother with Alice for a while and I knew all about it. As a daughter, my loyalty should've been with my mother and I could've told her about my father and Alice, but with the way she treated me, I really didn't care. Regardless of her dealings with my father behind my mother's back, Alice had always loved and protected me. She never condoned my father mistreating me.

She was more of a mother to me than my biological mother ever was, and I gave her more respect than I could remember giving to my mother. Alice made me feel seen and heard. She made me feel like I was special to her. When my mother died, it made sense for Alice to take on the role as stepmother. A role that she embraced.

I sat in my window on a late, summer night watching the streets, and all I could seem to focus on was my stepmother. I watched her get in and out of cars with strangers, collect money, and stuff it in her bra. At fifteen, I knew what she was doing was wrong, but I would never condemn her in my mind or out loud. The hopping in and out of cars lasted a few hours and I kept watch like her bodyguard in the distance. Not long after she had walked into the house, I could hear my father yelling at her.

"Where is my money hoe? Why is it short?!" His voice echoed through the walls. Alice matched his tone, screaming and hollering, making the situation worse. When I came out of my room my father was dragging Alice through the hallways. I watched as his open hand and closed fist connected with her face. He brutally assaulted her and ripped her clothes from her body. "Bitch, I knew you had my money!" He yelled as he continued his assault with a backhand across her cheek.

Alice always found ways to steal money in order to make sure that I not only had food on the table, but clothes on my back. She knew what she was risking by playing with my father's money, but she did it anyway. After making sure she handed over all of the night's take that she'd worked hard for, my father sent her to her room like she was a child. Satisfied, he left the house, and I immediately ran towards Alice's room. I swung the door open and flew into the room to be by her side. It hurt me to see her hurt.

"Are you okay?"

"Babygirl, I'm okay. You know I'll do anything to take care of and protect you," she proclaimed while holding my hand and looking into my eyes. I felt what she had said was true indeed. I'd always wondered why my stepmother protected me and loved me the way she did when I wasn't really her child. I planned to ask her one day when the time was right.

"Can I get you anything?"

"No Babygirl, just go to your room until I can figure everything out," she replied. I didn't know what she meant by that. I wanted so badly to stay with her in fear that my father would come back for round two, instead I did what I was told.

When he did return back to the house, I could tell that he was both high and drunk. He stood at the entryway of my room and told me he needed to talk to me. I stared up at him with disdain written all over my face as he spoke.

"Babygirl, what Alice did was out of line and I'm sorry you had to witness that. She's been stealing from me, and I finally caught her," he explained. I really wasn't trying to hear it. I knew what she did and didn't care because he deserved it. I sat on the bed and listened to him talk about nothing for a while, making up excuses as to why he needed to teach Alice a lesson, until she walked in. Her eyes were black, her lips busted and bloody.

My father looked over his shoulders and scolded her. "Get the fuck out, you fat bitch!" Him saying that to her broke my heart because I knew he was only being mean and hateful. Alice looked at my father with tear filled eyes and walked away from the door feeling embarrassed, I'm sure. I looked at him with disgust and shook my head. "You get you some rest and I'll see you in the morning." With that, he left my room and I laid my head on my pillow with thoughts of me and my stepmother getting away from him.

In the middle of the night, they were right back at it, but this time I didn't hear my father beating on Alice. I guess he figured she'd had enough. I could hear their heated argument through my halfway opened door. My father threw insult after insult at Alice and I didn't know how she had the strength to sit there and take it.

"Why did you marry me if you didn't accept me as I was, big and all?" I could hear her ask my father.

"I'm still trying to figure that out myself. I'm tired of fussing with you though. If you know like I know, you'll drop this and take yo' ass to bed. I'm still not over the fact that you've been stealing from me and I'm a few minutes off your ass." I only hoped that Alice took heed to what he said and left well enough alone. When I heard no response and saw my father walk past my room towards the back of the apartment, I knew she had.

Relieved, I laid back down and closed my eyes. Before I could get back to sleep, Alice rushed into my room. Her eyes darted around before landing on me. "Pack some of your things, we're leaving." I looked at her and smiled and then looked to my ceiling thanking God for answering my prayers.

Knowing we didn't have much time, I hopped out of bed and scrambled to grab as much of my belongings as I could. Once I was done, she motioned for me to follow her. We ran out of the door as quickly and quietly as possible. Throwing all of our stuff in the backseat of the car, we jumped in and sped off. Never looking back, we left both my father and Louisiana.

We found ourselves in Alice's hometown of Texas, where we moved from hotel to hotel, which was something I was used to. Even if I wasn't used to it, I didn't mind adapting. I was willing to do anything to stay away from my father. Being with Alice, I felt free, and I loved the thought of not having to worry about my father's verbal and physical abuse anymore. That feeling of being free ended all too soon.

One night while I was laying on the bed reading a book, I heard a loud noise. It was so loud, I knew it had to be right outside of our room. I got up from the bed and made my way to the window to see what was going on. My eyes widened when they landed on my father. I watched as he beat on a car window until it shattered. My heart rate sped up when I saw him reach inside the car and pull Alice out. He was yelling so loud, I could hear him all the way in the room.

"Bitch, you thought you could run to Texas, and I wouldn't find you?! You're on my turf and I have people all over this state. Where is Babygirl?" He barked. Alice didn't utter a peep of my whereabouts.

This only infuriated him, causing him to rain down heavy blows on her body. People went about their business as if the scene was a normal occurrence. Scared, I ran and hid in the closet. From the closet, I noticed the hotel door was slightly open. I had planted myself in the closet, frozen in fear. There was no way I could close it and risk being seen by my father.

I was slender in build, so it was easy for me to curl up on the closet floor to hide myself from his sight. The floor in the closet was filthy, but the thought of having to face him made me fight through it. My mind was racing and I had that terrible feeling in the pit of my stomach. I never wanted to feel this way again; at least not this soon. Memories of the night my mother was killed flooded my mind.

What if he killed Alice too? I thought to myself. I couldn't lose her. My thoughts were immediately cut short when I heard him bust into our hotel room. I could hear things being tossed around and concluded that he was trashing the place. It didn't sound like he was looking for me, in fact, he never even called out my name. He had to have been looking for whatever money he thought Alice had and drugs.

I had contorted my body in such a way that when he opened the closet door, he didn't notice me amongst the clothing that hung inside. I silently thanked God because if he had looked down, he would've seen me. Finding nothing, he left. When I heard him slam the front door, I let out a sigh of relief and waited for about five minutes before exiting the closet. Pushing the door open slowly, I picked up on how eerily quiet the room was. All of our belongings were thrown about the room and the mattress was turned over.

Rushing to the window in hopes of finding Alice outside, I panicked when I was unable to locate her. Fishing for my cell phone through the mess my father had made, I went to dial her number and paused. Alice had always taught me to think before I set my mind out to do anything. I knew that if she wasn't here then my dad had taken her and calling would be bad for the both of us. Here I was, a young girl, with no place to go, leftovers in the microwave, a few dirty clothes to put on, and no money.

I thought things like this only happened in movies, but reality had set in really quick that it was happening to me, and I had to accept it. I never knew my grandparents and I highly doubted any of my aunts would want me, so I opted to not call any of them. I was strong for the most part and Alice had taught me how to survive as best she could. I decided that I would wait to see how things played out. Taking my time to put the room back together, I listened to the radio for a while and wondered how many nights Alice had paid to stay in the room. I jumped up after the thought and rushed to the lobby. In such a rush, I almost fell walking in and the man sitting at the front desk giggled a little before asking me if I was okay.

"Yes, I'm fine," I replied, embarrassed. "I'm in room 212, and I need to know how many nights I have left to stay here before I have to pay again?"

"You should know that," he retorted. I ignored his smart comment. I wasn't in the position to go back and forth with this man, so I just waited for his answer. Looking down at the computer, he clicked a few buttons and looked back up at me. "It's paid for eleven more days." I sighed and thanked him, then turned to walk away. "If you need more time, I'm sure we can work something out, if you know what I mean." I heard him say from behind me.

I knew exactly what he meant and when I turned around and saw his creepy eyes staring at me with a mouthful of tobacco, I quickly made my exit. Back in my hotel room, I ran myself a bath to wash off the dirt from the closet as well as the old man's dirty stare. After taking an hour-long bath, I began to think of my next move. In the corner of the room, I eyed Alice's make-up bag, clothes, and Ziploc bag full of condoms. I knew I couldn't fit her clothes, but everything else was a go.

I was still a virgin, but I felt like it couldn't be that hard to use what I had to get what I wanted. Alice had sex for money every night and nothing happened to her. She returned home each night, with tired eyes but for the most part, she seemed alright. I mean, she was right back to it the next night like clockwork. I stood in the mirror, admiring my body, and the thought faded into my imagination. "No way," I thought to myself. "There has to be another way."

The next night as my stomach growled, thoughts of working the streets came back to my mind. With no money and no alternative, I got dressed in heels and the only dress that I packed. I put on red lipstick, put my hair in a high ponytail, and applied mascara and eyeliner just as I'd seen Alice do plenty of times. To look at the finished work, I grabbed the mirror that was left behind. I was amazed at how different and grown I looked.

Here it was a Thursday night, and I was about to do something I would probably regret later. I took one last glimpse at my innocent face and headed out the door. I didn't know the first place to begin so I turned and walked towards the lobby. The thought of that man at the front desk gave me the shivers, but I kept walking in that direction. Surprisingly when I stepped inside of the lobby, it was a woman standing behind the desk and not the pervert.

"May I help you?" The lady asked with a friendly smile. Looking down at my attire, I put my head down, ashamed, and walked out of the hotel without responding. Stepping outside, I was startled by a tall guy with tattoos that painted his neck. I admired his long beard and muscular frame. Figuring he could be my potential first customer, I shot him a seductive look as if I knew what I was doing.

"How old are you?" He asked.

"Eighteen," I lied. He asked me to get into his car and although hesitant, I followed as he walked in front of me. In my mind I was thinking, wow this is really about to go down. Sitting in the passenger seat, I avoided eye contact with him and went for what I knew and started to touch myself sexually. I leaned over and touched his face, still in disbelief that I was doing such things. I went to reach for the big bulge in between his legs, but he did something unexpectedly; he grabbed my hand.

"Why are you out here doing these things?"

Annoyed, I leaned back in my seat with an attitude. "Look, I'm just out here trying to make some money."

"Why?" He questioned further.

"Because I have to pay for my hotel room and buy food. Is there anything wrong with that, mista?" I clapped my hands at him. He pulled out a few hundreds and handed them to me. "What's the catch? And how can I repay you?" I asked with my eyes big in amazement.

"Just stay out of these streets, that's the catch. Next time, you won't be so lucky and run into somebody like me. You will get what you're looking for from one of these thugs out here." I slowly got out of the vehicle, embarrassed yet again.

How can I be so stupid? This had always worked for Alice, but I wasn't her. Heading back into the hotel, I made me way to my room. I wanted so bad to grab the phone and call Alice but I didn't want to regret calling. My dad may have been waiting by the phone or had her phone, and I couldn't risk it, at least not yet. Mulling over the night's events, I laid down and before I knew it, I was fast asleep.

CHAPTER TWO – BABYGIRL

The next morning, I woke up ready to get on my grind. I brushed my teeth, got dressed, and headed down to the lobby to pay for another full week at the hotel with the money the mystery guy from last night gave me. While paying, I asked the lady behind the desk if they were hiring. To my surprise, she replied yes and asked my age. Of course, I lied and said I was eighteen.

"Have you ever worked in housekeeping?" She asked me.

"Well, I clean my house really well. I believe that would be the same thing," I said, looking at her with hopeful eyes. My father was big on keeping his house tidy and being that I was the only one not out on the hoe stroll, my responsibility was to keep the house up. Waiting for a response, the woman just looked at me with a deep smile.

"Can you come back in the morning and speak with me or the other manager? Also be dressed to work?" I smiled and just like that, I had my first real job at the age of fifteen. I left the hotel elated that I'd taken a step forward. Heading towards the corner store, I planned to buy a few items with what was left of the money the tattoo guy gave me. I never got his name so I just called him "the tattoo guy."

As I made my trip to the store, I got stares from the people on the street that made me uncomfortable. It wasn't because they were staring at me in sexual manner, but because I knew my father knew many people. Alice had told me that her and my father met and began their journey in Texas. And if I knew anything about my father, I knew any new place we went, he made sure to make a few friends. Friends that wouldn't mind giving up information for the right price.

In the store, I bought things I could microwave back at the hotel, a few sodas, and water. On my way back to my hotel room, I kept looking over my shoulders looking for my dad's face. It felt like he would appear at any moment. I hated the fact that I was not only scared but paranoid. I had to keep telling myself that I was a survivor, and I was gonna make it through this.

When I got back to the hotel and put away my groceries, I decided that now may be a good time to reach out to Alice. Picking up the phone, I dialed the number and hung up before the phone call connected. I needed to wait and try calling her from a different number. I didn't want the number to the hotel showing up on her caller i.d. Being alone was the pits and although I was willing myself to be strong, I was still a young girl who needed guidance.

Unable to sleep, I got up and whipped myself up a meal. It wasn't the best meal, but it was decent for someone who wasn't skilled. I'd watched Alice whip up meals on the hot plate the hotel had available and stored a few recipes in my head. Although I'd purchased a few microwaveable meals, there was no way I could live off of that. Finishing my food, I stored what was left of it in the mini fridge. Downing a bottle of water, I laid down and forced myself to sleep.

The next morning, the alarm woke me up around seven a.m. from a deep sleep. I stretched and wiped the sleep from my eyes before finally reaching over and turning off the alarm. Getting out of bed, I headed for the bathroom to handle my morning hygiene which included a twenty minute long shower. When I got out of the shower, I realized that I had nothing to wear to my new job. Figuring that I was bound to get dirty anyway, I opted for a t-shirt and a pair of sweats. Brushing my hair up into a ponytail, I left the room, ready for the day.

"Wassup, do you have any spare change?" A random woman asked me in the hallway as I made my way to the lobby. I began to search my pockets, as if I may have had some change, knowing I had spent the rest of what I had at the store yesterday.

"I'm sorry, I don't."

The girl shrugged her shoulders. "It's cool. I'm Lily by the way."

"I'm Babygirl, nice to meet you," I said to her. We stood awkwardly for a few seconds before Lily turned and walked away without saying a word. I felt bad for the girl. I wanted to say more, but I had a job to report to, so I kept it moving towards the lobby.

"Hello, I'm Sarah. You are?" The lady at the front desk asked.

"I'm Cameron. I'm supposed to start the housekeeping position today," I replied.

"Oh yes, we were expecting you, Cameron. You have some paperwork that needs to be filled out, but we can do all of that later. You're going to be training with Tameka this morning, come with me." I followed Sarah in the back to what she said was the housekeeping stockroom where I was introduced to Tameka.

Tameka didn't seem friendly at all. In fact, she didn't even speak. All I got was a quick nod of her head. It was a good thing I wasn't here to make friends. I wanted to make my money and keep it moving. After the introductions, Tameka showed me the ends and outs of the job and even said I was a fast learner. This job was gonna be a cake walk. I knocked on one of my stayover doors, and Lily answered.

"Oh, hey Lily," I said in a friendly tone. "I didn't know you stayed here."

"Yep, I do," she answered, dryly.

"Okay, cool. Well, I work here now, do you need anything?"

"No, I'm okay," she replied before shutting the door abruptly. Not knowing what to make of the interaction, I shrugged my shoulders and went to walk away. The door swung open before I could turn my cart around.

"Hey, umm, Babygirl, will you let the front desk know that I will be checking out today? It turns out I don't have enough money to pay for another night. I'm going to take a shower and I'll be right out." I took in the somber look on her face and instantly felt bad for her. Little did she know, we were in the same boat.

"Okay, I'll let the front desk know Lily. It was nice meeting you, again." She nodded her head and closed the door. This time, she did it slowly. I could tell that whatever her situation was it was just as fucked up as mine.

Once I got off work, I went up to my room and went to close my blinds when I spotted Lily sitting outside, in front of the hotel. She had bags next to her, so I assumed she was waiting on her ride. I went to the door to check on her.

"Lily," I yelled out to her from the window, "why don't you come inside my room and wait on your ride?" She jumped up from the concrete slab with a smile and ran inside.

I giggled at her eagerness. "Be careful so you don't trip over your bags," I said as she entered my room. "How old are you, Lily?"

"I'm seventeen," Lily replied. "How old are you?" She posed the same question.

"I'm fifteen." I told the truth because she was around my age, and I felt comfortable. Although Lily looked older than seventeen, I took her word for it. "Where are you from?"

"I'm from Louisiana," I told her.

"Louisiana. What brings you to Texas?"

"I'll tell you later." I wasn't ready to tell my story of why and how I got here just yet.

"Oh, come on... tell me why you're here and where's your family?" She pushed.

"Well long story short, my dad is an asshole and my mom died when I was only eight years old, that about sums it up," I told Lily. We sat down and I passed her a plate of nachos that she devoured like it was her first and last meal of the day. I didn't stare at her though, wanting to give her space to enjoy her food. "So where is your family?"

"Well just like you, I was raised by a father and a mother who were both assholes and drug addicts. I ran away when I was your age, and just never returned home. No one has ever come to look for me, so I just stayed gone." Noticing her tears, I reached up and wiped her eyes.

"What's your next move?"

"I don't know, Babygirl. I live in hotels when I get enough money from prostituting. I'm pretty much in survival mode."

"Yeah, I tried my hand at that."

"Yeah, well how did it work out for you?" She questioned.

"Let's just say it just didn't work out and I figured that folding towels and cleaning rooms would suit me better," I laughed. I thought to myself, with both of us having it hard, why not just take the journey together. "Hey, what do you think about staying with me? I mean, we could put our money together and keep a roof over our heads."

"Really? I would love to stay with you as long as it won't be a burden on you. I don't want to invade your privacy," she said.

"What privacy? I'm fifteen, I don't have much of anything going on." I smiled.

"I could find a job and help out around here. Oh, thank you so much Babygirl." Lily reached out and wrapped her arms around my neck, giving me a tight hug. I assured her that everything would be okay because now we had each other. We both fell asleep talking about our plans.

"Rise and shine, it's already twelve o' clock in the afternoon. I made us both bologna sandwiches with cheese, YUM," Lily said jokingly. I rolled over with sleep in my eyes and stared at an energetic Lily.

"My body is so sore. Housekeeping looks easy but it's not. I'm so glad I'm off today," I said, struggling to get up. As I ate my food, I thanked her for the sandwich. "I think we're both overdue for a home cooked meal."

"Well, I can scrape up a few dollars and we can go out to eat tonight," she suggested.

"Girl, we can't afford it. Plus, we need every dollar we can get in order to keep up with the hotel bill," I replied, sounding like the more sensible one out of the two of us.

"Let me worry about the expenses and you just be ready tonight at seven o'clock," she said. It was clear she wasn't taking no for an answer, so I just nodded my head and smiled. "Wait, I have something to show you," she let out and reached over on her side of the bed where she slept. She picked up a paper shopping bag and dumped the contents of it out on the bed. There was two cellphones, clothes, and liquor sprawled out on the bed.

"Lily, where did you get all of this stuff from?" I asked.

"While you were sleeping like the queen that you are, I went out and got us these things," she said matter factly as if she had the money to do so. In my mind I knew the items were stolen, and that we were both headed towards some serious consequences. Still, I decided to put that to the back of my mind, live in the moment, and enjoy myself for once.

"I've never been out before so I guess this one time wouldn't hurt," I thought to myself. Going out in Texas was risky because anyone could be in contact with my father, but I threw caution to the wind and did it anyway. Later that night, Lily and I got dressed and took some shots of the Amsterdam she had bought. After taking my first shot, my chest was on fire and I immediately wanted to spit it out.

"Oohh, careful girl," she laughed, throwing back two shots of her own like a pro.

"Omg Lily, it's disgusting," I told her.

"Ahhh, you're a big girl. Come on, lets go."

We headed out the door to the cab that awaited us. Lily let me know that she knew the guy and had met him on a dating site. They flirted the entire ride. We were supposed to go to a restaurant, but she had other plans and we pulled up to a club. As I got a better look at the sign, I noticed that we were in front of not just any ol' club but a strip club.

She motioned for me to get out and instructed me to stand in the long ass line so that we had a spot. When she finally got to the line where I was, she told me that the bar and food was on her like she promised. She had done what she called a "quick trick" to get the money for us both to eat and drink all night. I handed her the fake id she had me hold in the purse that Alice had left behind and we moved up in the line.

"Damn, those girls are flexible," I pointed out to Lily as we entered the club.

"Yassss," she yelled over the music and pulled a few dollars from her bra to throw onto the stage. I giggled at her antics. When she hopped on stage with the strippers, my mouth shot open. The strippers cheered her on as she did a few dance moves, tooting her booty up in the air which could be seen through the mini shorts she had on. The DJ hyped her up through the microphone and we were both enjoying ourselves. She then hollered for me to join her on stage. Shy at first, I declined but after a shot of liquor she offered, I hopped on stage and started dancing in ways I never knew I could.

"Yes, bitch, I can get used to this," I told Lily.

"Huh," she asked, not being able to hear over the loud music.

"I said..." I started to yell out but figured she still wouldn't hear me, so I dropped it and kept dancing. When the song went off, everybody clapped for us and told us we worked the pole like professionals. A man dressed in a dark suit approached us, clapping his hands.

"Are you both employees of my club? If not, you should be. It's all about money and entertainment here at Debo's," the club owner said to us. Lily and I looked at each other and smiled. "What do you think about joining my team? I'm Debo by the way." He held his hand out and we both shook it.

"Nice to meet you," Lily and I said in unison.

"Are you both at least eighteen or older?" Debo asked.

"Well, yes of course," Lily spoke for the both of us. "When can we start?" She asked, licking her lips. I let her handle the conversation sceing as she was way more experienced in the streets than I was. I knew I could learn a lot from Lily.

"Next Thursday, Friday, and Saturday," Debo told us both. "Come check with me and we'll get you ladies set up. The rest of the night is on me. Consider it celebratory for the new job." It hadn't been 72hrs and already I had new employment.

After getting the good news, Lily and I had to keep our composure. We knew we couldn't be out here acting our age. I also knew that I was biting off more than I could chew and stepping into the lion's den. Life was moving way too fast for me and I knew it would only lead me to some trouble.

Available Now
on all online retail book platforms!!

OTHER BOOKS BY

URBAN AINT DEAD

Tales 4rm Da Dale
By **Elijah R. Freeman**

The Hottest Summer Ever
By **Elijah R. Freeman**

Despite The Odds
By **Juhnell Morgan**

The Swipe
By **Toōla**

Hittaz 1 & 2
By **Lou Garden Price, Sr**

Good Girls Gone Rogue
By **Manny Black**

The State's Witness
By **Kyiris Ashley**

Ridin' For You
By **Telia Teanna**

A Setup For Revenge
By **Ashley Williams**

COMING SOON FROM

URBAN AINT DEAD

The Hottest Summer Ever 2
By **Elijah R. Freeman**

THE G-CODE
By **Elijah R. Freeman**

How To Publish A Book From Prison
By **Elijah R. Freeman**

Tales 4rm Da Dale 2
By **Elijah R. Freeman**

Ridin' For You, Too
By **Telia Teanna**

Hittaz 3
By **Lou Garden Price, Sr.**

The State's Witness 2
By **Kyiris Ashley**

The Swipe 2
By **Toōla**

A Setup For Revenge 2
By **Ashley Williams**

Good Girl Gone Rogue 2
By **Manny Black**

Charge It To The Game 2
By **Nai**

Despite The Odds 2
By **Juhnell Morgan**

Stuck In The Trenches
By **Huff Tha Great**

BOOKS BY

URBAN AINT DEAD's C.E.O

Elijah R. Freeman

Triggadale 1, 2 & 3

Tales 4rm Da Dale

The Hottest Summer Ever

Murda Was The Case 1 & 2

Follow

Elijah R. Freeman

On Social Media

FB: Elijah R. Freeman

IG: @the_future_of_urban_fiction

Made in the USA
Middletown, DE
03 March 2023

25894046R00096